The Rio Verde Series

Book Three

Healing Hope

By

Elise Phillips

The Rio Verde Series

Book One: Restoration Road
Book Two: Fresh Faith
Book Three: Healing Hope

Dedication

For Misty, who reads everything first.

Table of Contents

Chapter One

I wanted to open the box as much as I didn't want to open it. I knew it was the letter from the lawyers—Coulter and Dixon—that had brought this on. It had pulled Teo back to the front of my brain again. Not that he really ever left the front of my brain. He just stepped aside for other things sometimes.

I stared it down, watching it loom above me from the top shelf of the closet. It was two in the morning. I had to work tomorrow. But it had been a day and I couldn't sleep because the box in the closet was demanding to be opened.

I knew why.

It was the letter. The lawyers. One lawyer specifically, Shawn Dixon. Dixon was new to town. Newish. Only been here for a few years. I was mad at him for his letter. He wanted me to come to the trial and play the grieving widow. He wanted me to be part of the spectacle. I didn't want to do it. I just wanted it all over.

I wanted the man who had killed Mateo in jail for the rest of his life.

I wanted to be able to stop thinking about him.

I wanted to move forward with my life.

Instead, I was going to sit on my bed, look at my dead husband's things, and wallow.

It had been a day.

I hadn't touched the big white box since I'd packed it up and put it away. Since I'd written *Teo* on it. It'd been up there for nearly a year. Gathering dust. I lifted off the lid and tossed it on the floor, and, pausing, took a deep breath. For a second, the room smelled like him again. It vanished quickly, gone too soon, leaving me more alone somehow.

1

On top was his high school football team t-shirt. On the back, it read "Baca" with his number—12. Rio Verde Tigers on the front. Next was his favorite jacket. A worn leather bomber twenty years out of style. He'd picked it up at a secondhand shop right before he'd decided to move back to Rio Verde. I always thought he looked so handsome in it. I knew one day Ria would love these old things of her father's. I'd tried to put myself in her shoes when I'd packed his things away. Tried to imagine what a teenage version of my toddler would want to have to help her remember her father. I hoped the shirt and the jacket would be good ways for her to feel close to him.

Beneath the clothes was our wedding album. It was what had been pulling me to the box. Those pictures. I pushed the box away and sat back against the pillows with the album.

Mallie and Isabel had put it together for us from photos all of the guests had snapped during the wedding and afterward at the reception. When all your guests carried cell phones, there was no need for a photographer. At least not for a wedding like ours. Casual and chaotic. Last minute. There was one of us standing at the altar, Will's father, Dr. Noah Bell, out of focus beyond us, Bible in his hand. Below that photo was a similar one. In this one, though, we'd been in our normal clothes, standing in a brightly lit courtroom before a judge. Our actual wedding nearly four months before the one at the church.

I smiled when I remembered how mad our parents had been when we'd revealed we'd eloped. My mom had said *dios mio* nearly a hundred times in a row. Dad had gone quiet and glared at Teo. Teo's parents had yelled. They'd always been more explosive than my parents. When we'd told them why we wanted to rush the wedding, the mood had changed again. I was pregnant. Ria, our honeymoon baby, was about to become a visible bump. It would have ruined the big fancy church wedding all of our family wanted.

Everything had been a race after our folks had understood. The wedding had come together in less than two weeks. I flipped through the rest of the book slowly, remembering every detail. Mallie and my mom altering my grandmother's wedding dress. Tres and Teo turning

Tres' then unfinished house into the site of our reception complete with a dance floor and thousands of twinkle lights in the trees. Even though we were already married the wedding had made it real. Made it public knowledge. It was like once everyone knew, our marriage could really start. All the photos were filled with so much happiness. I tried to hang on to it.

Could nearly three years of happiness last me the rest of my life?

I wish I knew.

An overheard conversation from earlier rushed to the front of my brain. It had ruined what should have been a good, fun evening with my friends—my family. We'd gathered for dinner and movies, to keep Mallie company until midnight when she started to fast for what would hopefully be a final surgery on her accident-damaged leg. Instead, I'd overheard my friends talking about me. I couldn't count the number of times I had caught people talking about me this past year. Always about me. Never *to* me. It was bad enough to catch strangers or people I barely knew talking about me. But to catch my friends, my family . . .

I'd frozen in the hallway, right outside of the kitchen where they'd gathered. I'd been with them just a few seconds before. They'd clearly thought I'd be gone longer.

"I think we need to do something." First my brother, Tres.

"You may be right. Luz isn't getting any better." Then one of my best friends, Joy.

"What can we do though? She's got to pull herself out of this herself, right?" My eyes darted to the doorway when a voice spoke. Will now. Will and I had known each other most of our lives. We'd had a rocky friendship but that was in the past. For some reason though, hearing him talk about me stung more than the first two. Probably because we'd worked so hard to build our friendship. It was so new. It felt like we'd slipped backward for a second. That our new friendship wasn't so solid after all.

"I didn't." The voice was soft but carried authority. Mallie. She understood what no one else could. "When my mom died, I didn't get through it on my own. Luz helped me. Tres, you helped me. Even you helped Will, and your dad, and my dad. Shoot, even Aunt Jo helped. I had acres of help."

"It's been a year, Mal. You weren't this bad a year out from your mom's . . ."

"I lost my mom, Will, not my husband. That is a whole different kind of loss. What would you do if you lost Joy?"

He didn't answer Mallie but I knew losing Joy would have destroyed him. Just like it would have destroyed Mallie if she lost Tres. Or if Tres lost Mallie. Or Joy lost Will.

Just like losing Teo had destroyed me.

I'd taken advantage of the pause in their conversation and made some noise, pretending to be on the way back from the bathroom, calling out that I was ready for dessert.

I'd pretended to be fine all night.

I had driven home slowly. Each intersection of the empty country road home was marked by a single light on a tall pole—an oasis of warm, amber light in the cold desert of darkness. I paused in each one, looking for other cars I already knew weren't there. No one was out at this time of night. I was alone in my beat-up car with the words of my friends swimming around in my head. *She isn't getting any better.* They were right. I wasn't.

I closed the album and my mind returned to my bedroom and the box of Teo's stuff. I put away the photos, the jacket, the t-shirt. Closed the lid and sighed. I looked away and stared up. Through the ceiling. Through the attic. Through the roof all the way to Heaven.

"Why did this happen?" Tears filled my eyes but I pushed through the swelling sadness and kept talking to God. "Why did You take him? Why did You let that horrible man kill him? Why him? Why our family? Were we too happy? Were things going too well?"

Silence was my only answer.

There was no sense of knowing or understanding. No voice from Heaven offering me comfort of guidance or even condemnation. Only empty silence. God had abandoned me with my grief.

Chapter Two

I must have slept. I didn't remember falling asleep. I didn't remember putting away the photo album and laying down on my pillow. When I woke, I was disoriented right away. The room was too bright; a trio of bulbs glared down at me from the slowly turning ceiling fan. The house was too quiet and my bed was full of Teo's things. The box I vaguely remembered packing away was tipped over, all his stuff scattered around again. For a bit I lay there, disoriented, the restless night slowly coming back to me. Wandering the house. Going through the box. Questioning God and getting no answers. I shook my head, clearing the cobwebs from my brain. Carefully I sat up, treasures from the box sliding across the bed as I moved. I put it all away in a rush. I didn't want to linger on it. I'd get sucked back in again.

Five hundred days. It had been over five hundred days. Seventeen months. I repeated the figure in my head over and over as I put away the box and made up the bed. Running my hand over the empty side of the bed. I had to keep reminding myself how long it had been. In the mornings my sleepy brain got confused sometimes. For half a second I'd forget and think it was all a dream. A terrible, terrible dream.

I turned away from the now-tidy bedroom, heading toward the kitchen, pausing to grab my cell. I pulled up my calendar as I got out a glass and poured myself some cranberry juice. One square on the calendar shone red, a beacon on the white digital landscape. I counted the days remaining until the red day. Nine. Nine days until the man who had killed my husband would go to trial. I didn't know what to feel. Anger. Excitement. Fear. Sadness.

"What am I supposed to feel about something like this?" I proposed the question to the empty kitchen. To God above. I studied the pattern in the countertop, playing a game in my head, trying to find faces or animals or shapes. I'd played it my whole life, always finding something in the abstract patterns. It soothed me. It was a constant. A distraction I could always count on to pull my focus off what was bothering me. This time it didn't work. There was nothing. No shapes in the blue, gray, and white swirls of the fake granite. No voice answering my question. No comfort. Only the empty, aching hole inside me, threatening to swallow me every day.

I jumped when the phone vibrated in my hand and a text message appeared. Only one person I knew would be up at five in the morning. Joy Abbott-Bell. Owner of Abbott Bakery. Supplier of the best baked goods in at least a four-county area. One of my very favorite people.

"I know you're up," the message read. "I know you haven't been sleeping. Come over to the shop. I'll feed you breakfast."

I smiled at the phone, warmed by the bossy message. Joy was a tiny force of nature. Red hair and tattoos and sugar and love. She'd changed the town when she decided to stay. Changed it even more when she married Will. She was something else and suddenly exactly the person I wanted to see this morning. I rinsed out my glass and headed to the bathroom. Hopefully, a hot shower and something yummy from Joy would finish chasing away the ghosts in my head.

*****

It took all of ten minutes to get from my house to the bakery at this time of morning. I missed having Ria in the car with me. Her car seat sat empty behind me. I loved my kid more than anyone or anything on this earth but a break from each other was always good. Being two had been hard on the both of us. I was looking forward to her turning three. Today I missed her sassy, grumpy self. It would be good to get her back from Mom and Dad in a while.

7

My stomach grumbled as I got closer to the bakery. Mornings with Joy had become a weekly routine. My stomach knew I was about to feed it much better than I normally did. Joy had gotten me hooked on her stuffed sourdough breakfast rolls. Warm sourdough bread stuffed with ham and cheese and sometimes green chilies. When I first tried one, Will had confided in me that the rolls, specifically the pizza version of them, had been the first thing about Joy he'd fallen for. He said his stomach had fallen in love first. After I'd had a few bites of a breakfast roll I was ready to steal Joy from Will. She was a goddess in a kitchen. She could do things with eggs, flour, and butter I knew had to be making God jealous. So I kept coming by for breakfast a couple of days a week. Ria had been an early riser from birth so it gave me a place to go with her where we could have a peaceful breakfast before the chaos at the diner started. Plus, Joy had a way with Ria. She could calm my child better than I could some days. I was secretly hoping she and Will would get pregnant soon. I couldn't wait for her to become a mama.

As my stomach grumbled a second time I turned again, taking my favorite detour. It was only a little out of the way—two whole streets—but I always felt like I had to drive through the historic district on my way to the bakery. It wasn't even a proper district although our mayor liked to call it one. It was really just three short streets of old houses. Fourth Street, where Mallie's dad lived, then Fifth, then Sixth, which led to the square at the center of town. I picked Sixth this morning. It was home to some of the biggest houses in Rio Verde. Many had been converted into duplexes or apartments. A couple housed businesses on the first floor and residences on the second. My favorite though was still a single family home that was still owned by the family who had built it.

I slowly took in the whole house as I got closer. Even in the dusty gray light of dawn and from a block away it was a stunner. Bright orange-red brick. Crisp, white trim. Steeply pitched roof with gingerbread accents. A tower on one of the corners on the front, rising up one story higher than the rest of the house. Gothic Revival—that's

8

what Mallie called it. If it had been painted in deeper colors and clothed in a gloomy dark brick or covered in ivy it would have looked like a haunted house. I had always thought it resembled a small church. It was, after all, tied to one of our churches. It had been built by one of the founding elders of the First Methodist Church, Hershel Tate. The Tate House shared a lot of architectural similarities with the big church on the southern edge of town.

He'd built the huge house for his huge family. I'd heard it had six bedrooms plus a guesthouse around the corner in the back. I'd never been inside though. The Tates were *the* big, important family in Rio Verde. Or they had been. Only one Tate still lived in the house and she didn't exactly invite folks over for dinner. Dad had told me they'd once held big dinner parties at the house. Fancy costume parties. Fundraisers for all sorts of causes. When Robert Tate was taken by a sudden heart attack, his wife Patsy stopped hosting anything. Stopped inviting anyone over. She didn't even get out much anymore. I saw her at the library sometimes but that was about it. Her kids, all older than me, had moved away to bigger, more exciting cities. I always felt sorry for her, on her own in the big old house.

I slammed on the breaks when I saw the sign. I felt a sippy cup crash into one of my feet and heard half a dozen things fall off the backseat but none of it mattered.

For Sale.

The Tate House was for sale.

Chapter Three

I sat in the middle of the road, staring at the Tate House and the realtor sign in the front yard until a light came on in the house. When a second one flashed on, it jarred me into motion. I hit the gas and headed right for the bakery. I couldn't wait to tell Joy.

I charged through the side door of the bakery, stopped myself, and looked back at my car. I'd turned it off. Good. The keys were probably still inside but I didn't care. My news was too big. My normal, entering-the-bakery routine was forgotten. No time to carefully park and lock up my car. No time to stop and take in the smell of freshly baked bread. No time to ring the doorbell. I was too excited by what I'd just discovered.

I just stormed into the kitchen and announced, "It's for sale."

I didn't bother with an explanation or a hello. Joy would know what I was talking about. She'd discovered the Tate House when she was jogging one morning when she first moved to town. She loved it too. It was a frequent daydream for us. We'd talk about what we could do with such a neat house. Joy had always said she and Will would fill it with kids. Ones they'd have. Ones they'd adopt. My kids. Mallie's kids. Her sister Lane's kids. Joy had grown up in foster care and in group homes. She wanted a family. A big happy family. She saw the Tate House as the perfect house for that family. My ideas had always changed. I'd thought about it as a family home but Teo and I hadn't really planned on Ria let alone having a house full of kids. I'd thought of businesses I could run from the Tate House. A fancy restaurant maybe. I'd never really settled on one thing. I'd wanted the house for reasons I couldn't name, I wanted the house to be mine. We hadn't talked about it once since Teo been killed. Our daydreaming had gone out of the world with him. Or at least mine had.

10

"I know. We saw it this morning when we went for a run."

"We? Didn't Will drive to Albuquerque this morning for the financial conference thing? How'd you get him to take time for a run?" Will was rigid about his fitness but he was even more rigid about all things business. He'd nearly driven straight to New Mexico from Tres and Mallie's house last night. It had taken all of us to convince him to go home and sleep for a few hours.

Joy smiled and looked up toward the second floor before opening one of the ovens and taking out a tray of what looked like big rolls of bread. Golden-brown, football-shaped domes of deliciousness. Breakfast.

"I didn't want to call you last night," she said. "I knew you'd stay late with Mallie. Carson's back."

It was the third time he'd drifted into town since Joy had gotten married. Since he'd missed Joy's wedding. None of us had met him. Well, Will had of course but no one else. He'd drop in for a day or two, she'd kind of disappear and hang out with only him, then he'd head out again, off to hike or camp or goodness knows what. I hadn't made up my mind on him yet. Had only seen him from across the square. I needed a face-to-face meeting with this guy. And, in all honesty, I was still sort of mad at him for not making her wedding. If they were as close as she claimed he should have been there. He'd helped her through getting sober and much more. It made me angry that he missed her wedding. There aren't many things more important in a person's life. Joy had pretended it hadn't bothered her but a friend notices things. I saw how sad she'd been.

"Yeah, he totally surprised us. Was waiting in front of the bakery when Will and I got home last night. He was stiff from driving all day so we went for a run first thing this morning. I wanted to show him around the town a bit. I nearly called you when I saw the sign but it was around four this morning."

I refocused on the Tate House, putting aside my feelings toward her wandering friend. Mallie told me I was judging him too quickly.

But Joy had become such an important friend and I was protective of her.

"I can't believe it's actually for sale. That house has never been out of the Tate family's hands."

Joy set the tray on a cooling rack, then grabbed a stack of plates, setting them on the marble-topped island in the center of the kitchen. I stowed my purse in her office and stepped up to help set out our breakfast. Joy's big cat, BC, appeared, meowing for attention. I had a soft touch for animals and scooped him up, cradling him like a baby. I was rewarded with a loud, happy purr.

"His breakfast is in the office if you want to feed him. Carson will be down in a sec."

When I came out of the office without the cat, the island was set for breakfast. Joy moved fast when she was hungry. I could smell other things baking now. Fresh bread was how Abbott Bakery started the day. Joy already had several loaves going in an oven and more resting on the counter, ready for their turn to bake. A sudden succession of heavy footsteps from the stairs followed by a crash in the hallway stopped me on my path toward food.

"That'd be Carson," Joy said, putting breakfast rolls on each of the waiting plates.

"Did he fall down the stairs?"

Joy smiled and chuckled. "No, Carson . . . creates noise. He's sort of like a one-man-band. He pounds up and down stairs. Hums or whistles. Taps his fingers or drums a pen."

"Sounds like he and Maria will have a lot in common. She started a new thing two days ago. Random squeals or screams then right back to what she was doing. It's great. She screamed bloody murder in the middle of the lunch rush yesterday and scared away two customers."

"You should totally fire someone for screaming at work." The statement made both Joy and I turn toward the side door of the kitchen. The elusive Carson LeBlanc in the flesh. It was the first time I'd been in the same room with him. He was taller than Joy but that

12

wasn't hard to be. She liked to tell us she wasn't short, she was pocket sized. Unruly locks of dark brown hair, still damp from the shower, crowned his head. Gray-green eyes watched me. He had a scruffy beard but a wore a friendly, bright smile.

"I can't fire Ria."

"Who's Ria?"

"My two year old. She's a screamer this week."

"Fun," he said climbing on to one of the stools around the island. He cast a lustful gaze on the still-steaming roll on the plate before him.

"Last week she threw things."

"Oh yeah," Joy said, claiming another stool. "Last week was fun. She nailed me right in the face with a stuffed bear."

I couldn't help but grin as I took the last seat. "The look on your face. I'm holding a picture of it in my head forever. It was priceless. Shock. Horror. Confusion."

"She normally loves me. I don't understand why she chucked the bear at me."

"Because she's two," Carson said.

"Exactly," I agreed. I reached for my fork but a look from Joy stopped me. To my surprise, Carson held out both his hands to us.

"Grace first?"

"Sure thing," Joy said, grabbing his hand and holding out her other hand toward me. I took their offered hands and closed my eyes and lowered my head. I hadn't had a meal prayed over since last Christmas. My family never missed a Sunday at church but praying over meals had never been a normal thing for us. Even Will, Mr. Preacher's Kid, didn't pray over meals. In our circle of friends praying over meals just wasn't the norm. I was surprised to learn so abruptly, so soon, that Carson was a religious man. Joy hadn't been a faith-filled person when she'd landed in Rio Verde. Knowing now that she had such a strong friendship with a religious man made me realize what a transformation her newfound faith really was.

"And thank You for letting Luz join us for breakfast today."

13

I looked up at Carson when he said my name but made myself concentrate on the rest of his prayer.

"And for blessing Joy with such a great friend. Thank you for this wonderful meal she's made us. Bless it to the nourishment of our bodies and our bodies to your service. Amen."

Joy and I echoed his amen as we all cut into our breakfast rolls. Cheese pooled on my plate and I sighed as the smell hit me. Sourdough bread, cheddar cheese, salty ham, sharp green chilies. Perfection.

"So Joy didn't properly introduce us but I know you must be Luz. Am I saying that right? A long 'u,' right?" I nodded and he reached out, shaking my hand quickly then turning to his breakfast. "Sorry it took me so long to get to meeting Joy's friends. This past year is the first time I've been in the southern part of the US in a long time. I've been busy bouncing around visiting friends and family."

Joy had never told me where Carson was from but when he spoke I caught a hint of a Cajun twang and guessed he'd at least grown up in Louisiana.

"Yup, I'm Luz and I owe Mallie twenty bucks," I said, speaking to Joy instead when she looked confused. When he didn't show up for the wedding, I told Mallie we'd never even get to meet him." I looked back to Carson, "I figured you'd never make it to little bitty Rio Verde. When you showed up, I amended my bet and said none of us would ever get to meet you."

"Mallie said y'all would?" Carson spoke around a mouthful of food, making Joy smile. It was a look I'd often seen my own sisters give our brother. Affection plus acceptance of his, in this case, poor table manners in the face of hunger.

"She did. She had faith that you would stay put long enough for a proper visit with all of Joy's new friends. She even thinks you'll fall in love with the town and stay, like Joy did."

"Well, I officially like this Mallie person then. You, on the other hand, chère, you're going to have to find some faith in me. And both of you are going to have to show me around your town. If it can

14

get the great, always-wandering Joy Claire Abbott to put down roots, it's got to be a pretty amazing place."

I couldn't help but laugh. He was funny and frank and, surprisingly, a man of faith. I decided right then to like him. I didn't really have a choice, I realized. Like Joy, he was one of those people you were instantly comfortable around. She'd instantly been someone I wanted to be friends with, even though she took a bit longer to decide that. I had a feeling Carson was the same way. I laughed again when Carson reached his fork over to Joy's plate, snagging a bite of her food. She smacked his hand without missing a beat. Today felt like the first time I'd really laughed and relaxed since Teo had been killed. Even last night, hanging with my friends, having fun, I hadn't been able to shake the clinging sadness. In that moment, laughing again as he teased Joy, I liked him even more for giving me a reason to laugh for a second or two.

*****

By the time we'd finished our breakfast, the other bakery employees had arrived, turning the quiet kitchen into a noisy, busy bakery. Joy's mom had charged in, giving us all hugs before going out front and opening the blinds, turning on the lights, and unlocking the front door. Joy's half-sister Lane rolled a partly assembled cake out of the walk-in freezer as soon as she put on her apron, getting right to work on what looked like a child's birthday cake. Gia, the only non-family member of the crew, started measuring out ingredients, turning on one of the big industrial mixers. She was the newest member of the bakery staff. It had been rocky for her at first, joining a family-owned and family-run business. She'd become part of the family right away though.

Carson and I were instantly very much in the way. He fled upstairs as fast as he could, muttering about needing to shave. I knew I needed to go too. I needed to start the same sort of ritual at the diner on the opposite side of the square. I couldn't bring myself to leave

15

though. Lately, the Red, White, and Blue Diner was the last place I wanted to be. I felt my folks and my sister Marisol watching me, waiting to see if I was better or worse every single day. It was like living under a microscope and it was exhausting.

When I saw the lights come on in the diner, I gave in and started to gather up our breakfast dishes. Joy stopped me, tugging me into her office instead.

"Did you get one of these?" She held up a certified letter with a familiar return address—the law office roughly one hundred steps away.

"Yeah. What did yours say?"

"They want me to testify. They said what happened to me speaks to the character of . . . that man." Joy looked away from me, staring at the letter in her hand instead. I knew what she was thinking. I was thinking it too. Remembering what had happened nearly two years ago. The man who'd killed Teo had, with another man, beaten her so badly she'd ended up in the hospital when they had robbed the bakery. It had been terrifying for all of us but just a pit stop on the crime wave the two men and created that year.

"Are you going to?"

"Yes. I wasn't at first. I want to forget about all the . . . all the . . . badness he did in our lives. Will talked me into it though. He thinks I can help make sure he gets convicted. What did they want you to do?"

"Come. Come and sit in the front row with Maria and play the grieving widow." It made me furious saying it out loud. "I want to call them and tell them no. I'm don't want to let them leverage Mateo's death. Use my grief like that. It's cruel of them to even ask me to do it." I looked away, like Joy had, staring at the letter she held. I'd stared at my own copy for hours when it had come. I wanted to stop reliving what had happened. I wanted to move past it all but this trial wouldn't let me. It had loomed over me for months and months. I couldn't get free of it. Going, sitting there, playing the part they wanted me to play

. . . it would put me back into that terrible night again. I couldn't do it. I just needed it all to be over, finally.

Joy gave me a sad smile and squeezed my hand. "I was afraid they'd ask you to do something along those lines. You should listen to your gut and tell them no. Don't put yourself through it. Do you want me to keep you updated about the trial?"

"No. I don't know. Maybe. I just want it over. I want it all over and done with. I want him to go to jail for the rest of his life and I never want to think about him again. I want this all to end, I want to be able to stop thinking about it every day."

"I'll do my best to make sure that happens." She hugged me again then let me escape. I was across the square and in the diner by the time Dad had turned on the neon open sign. The familiar jingle of the front door bells announced my arrival.

"Breakfast with Joy?" Dad headed my way, Maria in his arms.

I reached out for her as he spoke and he handed her off, heading toward the kitchen. I followed him, hugging Ria close, breathing in her familiar little kid smell, the special perfume of Cheerios, baby powder, and diaper cream. I'd missed my kid.

"Yeah. She always knows when I can't sleep."

"She's a good friend to you," my mom said as she came out of the office, cash bag in hand. She stocked the register with bills and change, watching me out of the corner of her eye.

"Yup. I'm a lucky girl." I couldn't help but remember the conversation I'd overheard last night. I didn't feel so lucky. I felt . . . something else. Judged for my grieving, for my lingering sadness, for my not-right-ness. Breakfast with Joy had been good and getting to know Carson had been great. But now, away from them, the feeling the overheard conversation had given me returned. I couldn't name it—I wanted to call it betrayal but that felt too harsh. It was something else. Something I didn't like feeling about my friends.

We chitchatted as we opened up for the day. Mom and Dad settled into the kitchen, getting our breakfast menu started. I put the coffee on and put pitchers of water and orange juice in the fridge, balancing Ria on my hip while I worked.

Before long customers started to trickle in, several regulars offering to hold Ria for me. My baby sister Marisol raced in as soon as her morning class let out and stepped in to help me wait tables, catching the end of the breakfast rush. It was a busy day from the start. A welcome distraction from everything going on in my head. Tres called right before lunch to let us know Mallie's knee surgery had gone well. I could hear her in the background asking for coffee so I knew she was feeling fine.

All day as I worked and took care of Ria and helped Marisol with her homework, I thought of the Tate House. It sat in the back of my head all day and all night. A big house and a for sale sign. The dreams Joy and I'd once talked about came back to me. The house was possibilities. Possibilities and a future I hadn't thought about in a year. I felt like I'd gotten something back. Some spark inside of me that had been missing. By the time Ria's bedtime rolled around I knew what I had to do. I had to buy the Tate House. I didn't know why. I didn't know what I'd do with such a huge house. I knew, really knew, I was supposed to have that house.

Chapter Four

My heart hurt.

For a moment, I let myself feel it all. I kept the pain at bay most of the time. I'd learned to go on and move forward. I'd learned to get back to doing life type stuff again even if I was running on autopilot. Today though it was flooding me. Another important moment Teo was missing. Will's birthday. Not a huge deal but Teo had always loved a good party. Next year would be mile-stone birthdays for several of us. Mateo's big sister, Tia, would be thirty-five. Marisol would be twenty-one. Mallie and I would each be turning the big three-o, her in June then me in July. Thankfully, Tres and Teo had gotten to celebrate their thirtieth birthdays together the year we'd married. I was glad they'd gotten to have that big birthday together. I still wished he had been here for this year's round of birthdays. And for all the other big and small things he'd missed this year.

From my spot in the dark, empty diner I could see both floors of Abbott Bakery blazing with light. I could see people I knew and loved walking around through the big windows. I could even see my own daughter being carried around by family and friends. It was a happy party in full swing but my heart still hurt. I didn't want it to but tonight my old grief had just floored me, knocking me down as I'd gotten ready to go.

I was supposed to be over there. I'd closed up The Red, White, and Blue an hour ago. Sent my folks and Marisol across the square with Ria. I'd stayed behind to finish up the day's work. I'd balanced the books, gotten the night deposit ready, and cleaned everything I could think of to clean. It felt like my last day at the diner. Since I had settled on the idea of buying the Tate House the day before, something in me had shifted and changed. I was excited about the new options

19

the Tate House represented. At least I had been until I'd gotten to work. Then I'd started to think about leaving the diner. Not working with my family every day. Then my excitement had faded and the day hadn't felt like a normal day at work anymore. It had felt like an ending.

Between the sense of finality and the missing-Teo blues that had recently returned, I wasn't in a party mood. So I was stalling. I needed to soak up the quiet for a while. Shore myself up again. Pull it together. I couldn't handle overhearing Tres and them talking about me again. I was as sick of myself as they were. Hearing them talking about me though . . . it didn't help things even a little bit. When I'd overheard them it had made me feel like I was disappointing them, letting them down by not getting past everything fast enough. I felt like I was failing at being a widow or something.

Maybe they did help though. I was having a good talk with myself. I was thinking about things in the future for once.

The truth was I was sick of being sad and grieving. I wanted to be happy again but I just couldn't seem to shake it. Teo wouldn't want me to keep walking through life like a shadow. I wanted to get back to living. Our little girl deserved a mom who wasn't going through the motions like a ghost. I gave myself ten seconds longer to feel this most recent wave of grief and then I grabbed my purse and headed out, pausing to lock the diner behind me. The trip across the grassy square was quick. I detoured to the bank just two doors down and slipped the bank bag into the night drop-off slot. Then, after taking a deep breath, I headed into the loud party in the bakery.

"Luz!"

The bellow of my own name caused all the people in the room to turn and stare at me for a half second. I smiled and waved at the room and the spotlight shifted off of me once again. Joy barreled toward me from out of the crowd.

"Joy!" I hugged my friend, smiling when her husband appeared and hugged us both. "Happy birthday Will!"

I took a moment to look at them. They were such a mismatched pair. Tall and short. Light and dark. Tidy and messy. They fit though, fit perfectly. Their differences balanced out. I thought of Tres and Mallie; they fit perfectly too. Mallie with her careful planning and Tres with his let's-see-what-happens enthusiasm. I missed having someone I fit with. Joy broke the moment before I could get sad. She caught my arm and tugged me through the gap between the bakery display cases and into the white and stainless steel kitchen.

"Eat," she demanded, handing me a plate with a generous slice of cake on it. "We cut it already but saved plenty for you." I stared at it for a second, taking it all in. Three layers of snowy white cake with layers of pale yellow icing between them and more icing on top. I smelled lemon and sugar and probably a bit of Heaven. Everything Joy baked could make angels sing.

I tried to say thanks over a mouthful of cake as Mallie appeared beside me, speaking for me.

"She says thank you and that I can have half of her slice." She grabbed a handy fork and tried to steal a bite.

I slapped her hand away. "Get your own cake."

"She's had her own slice already," Joy said. "Mallie has a cake problem."

Mallie laughed and leaned against the counter. Even one day post surgery and on crutches, she wouldn't have missed Will's party. Family was everything to her.

I forced a laugh of my own and kept eating, watching my best friend. She looked good. Short blond hair fixed and tidy for once. No beat-up work clothes tonight, instead she'd put on a long skirt and a sweater. Mal looked happy but also very tired. I could tell her knee was hurting. She was paler than normal and leaning heavily on her crutches. Tres was hovering nearby too, watching her closely. His blue eyes were narrowed with worry as he kept an eye on her. I knew she was probably here against her doctor's orders. It didn't surprise me one bit. No one really ordered Mallie around.

21

A boom of laughter pulled my focus away from Mallie and I turned my attention to the front of the bakery. It was full of people. I watched the crowd for a bit, thinking. I saw the bakery every day from my family's diner across the square. I knew how busy it had become since Joy had taken it over almost two years ago. An idea popped into my head.

"You should think about expanding. The hardware store next door never has any business. You could buy it and expand," I said. "You're busy Joy. Crazy busy."

Joy smiled and boosted herself up on the counter across from me. "I am crazy busy. I'm hiring another baker as soon as I can find someone. I have more work than the four of us can handle. We're getting business from every town within fifty miles. It's nuts."

I looked back into the bakery as she spoke, quickly spotting the people she'd spoken of. Her mom, an older version of Joy, stood in the corner by an old record player, chatting with Joy's father. Since they'd reconnected and mended things between them, Joy had gotten what she'd always wanted—her parents. They'd started dating recently. The third redhead in the bakery was easy to spot. Joy's younger half-sister Lane, although the half part didn't matter at all; she and Joy had a bond just like I had with my own sisters. Lane laughed at something Carson had said and the fourth member of the Abbott team stepped into view, laughing too. Gia, a single mom with strawberry blond hair in a long braid and heavy, black-framed glasses. She always looked more like a computer nerd than a baker to me. The four women had made the bakery a shining star in our little town. Even though expanding would probably work great I didn't think Joy would do it. She loved the small bakery and the personal touch it allowed her to give every single thing coming from the kitchen.

I looked back at her as she chatted with Mallie and I finished the huge and divine slice of cake. Studying Joy, I wondered where her baking skills came from. She looked like a normal person but she was magic. A magician with sugar and flour. Joy laughed and suddenly she looked different to me. I couldn't put my finger on how so I kept watching her while I scraped the cream cheese frosting off my plate. She hopped off the counter, hugged Mallie goodbye and sent her and Tres out the side door of the bakery, still looking like not-quite-normal-Joy. When she came back, she caught me watching her. She cocked her head, trying to read me, but her mom appeared in the bakery doorway and that shifted her attention. And then I caught it. An unconscious gesture. One I knew well. She'd placed her hand over her belly for a second. I'd done the same thing a hundred times when I'd been pregnant.

"Luz..." Joy warned me when she looked back and saw the realization on my face. "Don't . . ."

"Don't what? Have more cake? Because you're not the boss of me, Joy Abbott. I'm having more cake."

As I headed back out front in search of more cake she caught my arm and whispered thanks. She didn't need to worry though. I wouldn't have stolen the moment from her. Joy was still figuring out what it was like to have a close circle of friends. She'd been in Rio Verde roughly two years and was still learning how to stay in one place. Growing up in foster care hadn't given her the best people skills or friendship experiences. She'd told me not long ago that she still had a little voice in her head whispering to run some days. I was sure though that the baby in her belly would silence that voice for good.

Chapter Five

I found the job site easily but only after I'd called Mallie for directions. Will's birthday party had made it clear to her she needed to actually listen to her doctor for once so she was home in bed, resting like she was supposed to be. She'd given in to exhaustion and pain, Tres had told me, finally admitting she needed to actually take the pain medication she'd been prescribed. I hadn't been surprised when she'd given in this morning. She was right on schedule. Two days out from surgery was about the same amount of time it had taken her to stop toughing it out after her last knee repair. She was predictably stubborn.

Tradition was continuing on without her. When she and her dad had started their restoration business, my parents had started sending out lunch for the whole crew toward the end of the project to celebrate. Now each time Andrews and Andrews Restoration was a week or two out from finishing a job, I packed up bags and bags of burgers and fries, grabbed a case of bottled water, and headed to the house they were restoring. This time I was headed to an old ranch house well outside of the city.

The house was a long, low building with a deep, shady porch stretched across the front. Mallie had texted me pictures of it when they first started. The front porch hadn't been there at all. The house had been weathered down to bare wood siding and had been about half the size it was now. They'd added on a whole wing for a big kitchen and a master suite. I saw the new section as I pulled around to the side and parked my car. As always, they'd done an amazing job. The addition was seamless. A stranger would never know the house hadn't always been so big.

I stepped out of my car and opened the back to gather the food.

"Luz Baca, what are you doing at my job site?"

I smiled at the bellowed question. Mallie's dad. My Tio Jonah. He asked the same question when I came to his house. Or when I ran into him at Mallie and Tres' house. Or even when I bumped into him at Walmart or at church.

"Hola, Tio. I brought y'all lunch."

He smiled, hugged me, and started lifting boxes out of my car. I followed him as he made the rounds, handing out the lunches as I handed out bottles of water. Jonah had been a fixture in my life from before I drew my first breath. My dad's childhood best friend. Lifelong best friend really. Dad and Jonah had been walking side by side through life since they'd become friends in first grade. As I was growing up, he'd been more present in my life than either of my parents' actual siblings. He and his wife, my Tia Tess. Thinking about her made me miss her all over again. It didn't seem as though she'd been gone four years. My parents had been right when they'd warned little-kid me that time flew by when you got older.

"You're staying and having lunch with me," Jonah said. I pulled my brain back to the present and looked up at him. We'd made it all the way around the job site and still had two sack lunches. Mom. She must have wanted me to stay out here and take a break from the diner. Since I'd lost Mateo, she'd made sure I had time with Jonah. He'd been an anchor for me. The only person I could talk to about this kind of a loss. At least he'd been lucky enough to get more time with her. They'd been married over thirty years when she'd been killed.

"Looks like I am." I took two bottles of water, leaving the last of the case on the hood of my car. I knew some of the guys would want another bottle. The leftovers would be long gone by the time I came back. I followed Jonah again, this time away from the crew, over to his pickup. He'd parked in a sunny spot so we sat on the open tailgate, enjoying the bright November day.

"How are you holding up, Luz?" he asked as he bit into his burger.

I took a bite of my own, stalling for a second. My armor must have cracked. I'd gotten so good at convincing people I was fine. Of course, Jonah had known me since I was an infant. He always saw things other people missed.

"I'm okay I guess. I'm not sure everyone else agrees though."

He gave me a look. It said so much. *Oh really? Who thinks that? How do you know?* It was amazing how much he could say without saying anything.

"I overheard them all talking about me, the other night before Mal's surgery. They think I'm worse and I should be better now."

"Are you worse?" he asked over a mouthful of fries.

"I don't think I am. I'm not more sad or anything. It's just . . . the trial starts soon."

"Tres told me. He said he's going to be there every day. Already has a guy hired to finish up with the hay crop so he can be there and not worry about getting all the hay stored for the season."

"I knew he'd be there." My brother and Teo had been friends for nearly their whole lives.

Jonah gave me another look. There was only one question in it this time: *Will you?*

"I can't go. It makes my heart start pounding to think about it. I don't know what I'd do if I was face-to-face with . . ."

"Did I tell you I met the person who caused Tess' wreck? I wanted to punch him. He showed up at the house one day, about six months after she passed. I wanted so badly to scream at him and beat him until I felt better. Instead, I sat on the front porch with him and listened to his apology. He'd been rushing his daughter's horse to the vet that day. The poor thing had gotten spooked and ran through a wire fence. It was cut to ribbons. His daughter had been sobbing in the front seat beside him. He had been driving in a blind panic, terrified the horse would bleed out before they got to the vet. He never even knew he'd cut someone off and caused a wreck until a few days later."

"You never told me. Did you tell Mallie?"

"I did, just recently. She wasn't ready to hear it for a while."

I nodded, returning to my quickly cooling food. Mallie had eaten herself up with guilt over her mother's death. She and Tess hadn't spoken in months when Tess died. After Mal finally forgave herself, she turned her anger toward the driver who had caused the wreck. It took her a lot of talks with God to get through everything she'd had churning inside.

"Did the horse make it?" I finally asked. I didn't know why, but I needed to know. For some reason, I needed the horse to be okay.

"It did. The girl took it to the state 4-H show this year."

I nodded again and smiled. "Good. I'm glad."

"Me too, kid." Jonah hugged me hard then hopped off the tailgate. "Back to work. Tell your mom thanks for the food."

"I will. Love you, Tio."

"Love you too, Lucy."

I watched as he walked back to the crew. Everyone stood as he approached, ready to go back to work. As always, talking to Jonah gave me hope. He got through it. With faith and help from everyone who loved him, he got through it.

I could too.

Chapter Six

"Joy told me what happened."

Carson's statement caught me off guard. He, Joy, and Will had been the last customers at the diner tonight. I'd been cleaning up when I'd heard the bell over the door jingle. I'd assumed it had signaled all three of them leaving. I hadn't looked up or called out goodbye, keeping to my work instead. I hadn't thought Carson had stayed behind. I stopped mopping and turned toward him. He was sitting at the counter, a half-empty glass of ice tea in front of him. Just watching me. I felt my face warm and looked away, rolling the mop bucket to the next section of dirty floor.

"Oh yeah?" I knew I needed to respond and it was all I could come up with. A pitiful response. A grumpy response. I chided myself. I needed to do better with Joy's friend. I reminded myself of breakfast the other morning. I remembered laughing while we ate, Carson making me laugh, and I reminded myself that I liked him. He was not the reason I was worn thin today. No one was. I was just worn out with the world and tired but I could suck it up a bit longer and be nice to my new friend.

"Yeah. She knew I would relate to it."

I thought about what he said. The seconds stretched out, the only sound the muted clatter from the kitchen as Dad did his share of the cleanup. Mom and Marisol were in the office getting the bank deposit ready while Ria—hopefully—kept on sleeping. The quiet after closing was my favorite part of the day. I thought about how, once, I'd hated the end of the day. Hated seeing the customers leave. Then Carson's statement finally registered in my tired brain.

"Wait, what?"

"I relate to it. I've been there. Been where you are now."

"What do you mean? Are you always this cryptic?"

Instead of answering he took a long drink of ice tea. I watched, waiting for him to answer me. I knew he was trying to become friends. He'd been trying since we'd had breakfast together last week. I'd decided that it really had bothered him when I had said I didn't think he'd ever come to Rio Verde. He seemed determined to win me over now.

"You want to get some air?" he said as he set the glass down. "Maybe go for a drive? We should talk. I think, maybe, I can help you out."

It wasn't the answer I'd expected, but the moment he said it all I wanted was to get out of the RWB for a while. I nodded and leaned the mop against a table.

"One sec," I said as headed to the kitchen. I told Dad I was running an errand and would be by the house to get Ria in a while. He nodded and waved me off. I knew I'd have to explain later but for now, I was happy to get out of there for a bit.

"Lead the way."

I followed Carson out the front door and into the dark street. He'd parked right around the corner, under a streetlight. I was able to give his dark green Jeep a once-over as we approached thanks to the halo of light around it. Joy had told me Carson had spent most of the last ten years crisscrossing North America in the thing. Backpacking, working when he had to, wandering wherever the wind took him. I hadn't created a picture of it in my head but I was surprised anyway. It didn't look like a vehicle that had crossed a continent several times over. Instead, it was simply a clean, well-cared for old Jeep. No national park bumper stickers or logos for whatever brand or coffee shop was trendy now. Just a simple forest green Jeep. Fabric cab and missing doors he would probably regret when winter hit in a week or three. A little wear and tear on it but it was in way better shape than it should have been. It was in way better shape than my own car.

Once I climbed inside I was surprised again. On the dash were two bumper stickers. Both had been faded by the sun but the words were still clear. One was a verse from Proverbs that read, "We can make our plans but the Lord determines our steps." The other was a quote from Martin Luther that said, "God writes the gospel not in the Bible alone, but on trees and flowers and clouds and stars."

"You know, most people put those on the outside of their car. Like on the back bumper."

He smiled, turning the key and pulling away from the curb. "I know, but if they're in here I see them constantly. Keeps me centered on what's most important in this world."

I hadn't known what to expect of Joy's infamous Carson but the reality was a turning out to be a surprise. I'd had a picture in my head of a kind of hippie guy. A nature-loving, yoga-doing, vegetarian type of a person. Not the simple, kind, Godly man he was turning out to be. I was starting to understand why he was Joy's anchor. Or why he had been. She seemed anchored by other things now. I still wondered how his very obvious faith hadn't worn off on her all the years they'd been friends. Joy, however, was impressively hardheaded. Maybe the magic I'd always believed Rio Verde harbored had been what she'd needed to crack her hard shell and plant the seed of faith her life had been missing.

Carson and I drove in easy silence for a while, my mind busy, following thought after thought as I wondered about the near stranger beside me. He wandered through the dark town, hitting the countryside in hardly any time at all. He picked a dirt road at random, leaving behind the blacktop in a cloud of dust. I recognized the area and started to direct him.

"Take the next left."

"Why?"

"Trust me."

He listened and after a couple more turns we were climbing up in the moonlight, leaving behind Rio Verde. At the top of the hill, the road branched off, the main section continuing on, the other dead-ending at a sagging barbed wire gate. Carson pulled up to the gate without prompting, then turned off the Jeep and climbed out. I followed him quickly.

"Wow. I've never paid attention when I've driven in town. I had no idea the city was in such a neat little valley."

I could have explained to him the geography of the area and the whole Texas panhandle. Told him about the Caprock and the canyon systems. Given him a lesson on the Texas high plains. Anyone who had grown up here knew it all by heart. It made our part of Texas special. I didn't say anything though; instead, I walked through the short grass to get a better view. Below us, the features of the valley were painted in shades of gray and black, barely visible in the early November night. The city was a network of twinkling lights in the center. A few days earlier and we'd have been able to see the lights from the yearly Halloween carnival.

"I love this view," I finally said, sitting down in the grass. "The lights remind me of my wedding day. My brother hung tiny white lights above the outdoor dance floor. There were thousands of them, tiny stars above us while we danced. The city lights flicker and shine like those lights did."

"A *fais-do-do*," he said as he stood beside me.

"A what?"

"A dance party. That's what it's called down in the Big Easy, back home. A *fais-do-do*. It roughly means to go to sleep. Doesn't make much sense but most of the slang down there doesn't."

"I like that. It sounds more fun than just calling it a dance." I looked away from him, back toward the city lights. I closed my eyes and for a second I pictured my wedding night, dancing with Mateo under the twinkle lights.

"You come up here a lot?" Carson sat beside me, running a hand through his messy hair, then stretching out his long legs with a sigh.

"Not here in particular, but yeah. I like to drive out of the valley and sit for a while, watching the world go by. I don't have much time for it but when I can, I slip away for a little while."

31

"It's peaceful. Thanks for steering me here. I may take a page from your book and come up here every now and then."

The "every now and then" surprised me. It sounded like he was staying. Staying-for-good staying. I wondered if he realized he'd said it. I looked at him out of the corner of my eye. He was relaxed, looking off into the night. He didn't look like he was planning to leave. He looked settled. I hoped he would stay. It would make Joy happy having him around and give me a chance to really get to know him.

For a while we sat, watching the headlights of cars and trucks appear and disappear among the groupings of now invisible trees. It'd been a warm day, unusual for right after Halloween. I soaked it in, letting the warmth left in the sun-warmed ground anchor me, as the air rapidly cooled around us. From our spot, we couldn't hear any cars or noises from people. It was the silent prairie, an occasional coyote yip, and little else.

"What did you mean, back at the diner?" The waiting was wearing on me. He'd seemed so eager to talk earlier. I hoped that now, away from everyone—and everything—else, he'd answer me.

"I get what you're dealing with." He went silent for a moment and I turned my head, watching him. He'd left the parking lights of the Jeep on and in their dull, golden light I could see his dusty green eyes looking at things that weren't there. Sadness settled over his face and my stomach dropped. "Right after high school, I hit the road, leaving New Orleans for cooler weather and a new life—I was dying to see more of the world than the swamps and bayous. I had grown up doing odd jobs on fishing boats so I had this great idea that I could go to Alaska and get the same sort of work up there. I got lucky and got hired on a crab boat. I got even luckier when I got an apartment in Seward after the crab season ended. I didn't want to be one of those seasonal guys. I wanted to live up there and become an Alaskan—I had this need to purge the Louisiana from myself. I got a new job in a processing plant and settled into living in Alaska full time. Then I met a local girl and fell hard for her. We were married less than a year later. We made it five years."

Carson's words hung in the air. I knew what he was going to say and my heart was already breaking for him.

"She was killed in a car accident. She was pregnant. I was driving. I'd been drinking, something I'd done a lot of since I'd moved up there. Alaskans like to drink and party, crab fishermen even more. The accident wasn't my fault, even though I know the alcohol slowed my reaction time. Another car hit a moose then lost control on the icy road. They crossed the double yellow line and hit us head-on. The airbag saved me. It didn't save her or our son."

I wanted to reach over to him, cover his hand with mine or something else to offer comfort. I stayed still though. I didn't know him well enough to know how to comfort him. I understood losing a spouse. But losing a child—I couldn't even fathom it. I didn't know if I could have come back from something like that.

"I can't imagine."

"Yeah. It was pretty awful. I disappeared into a bottle for a while. Then a buddy told me he was going to go hike the Pacific Crest Trail, start in Canada and hike the whole way down to Mexico. I didn't have anything else going for me so I said I'd go with him. The hike got me sober. There aren't a lot of liquor stores on the trail. Plus my buddy was a preacher. He shared his faith with me while we hiked. He taught me about God's forgiveness and grace, about Heaven and life after this world. His faith helped me grow my own. It saved me and set my life back on track. I kept hiking after that; it took me a while to get my head totally clear. Cities were a trap for me for a while. They were places where it was too easy to grab a beer and then another one and get lost. Things are clearer when you get away from all the noise and temptations. I tried to share all the things I'd learned with Joy when we became friends. It's why I invited her to hike the Appalachian Trail with me. She wasn't quite ready to hear all the God stuff but it did at least help her get sober."

I didn't know what to say. Joy had told me he hiked for bigger reasons than the fun of hiking. I understood it now. He had hiked through his grief. If he'd made it through a loss so like my own, then hopefully I would too. I needed to find something to help me through this. Going through the motions of normal life wasn't working. I constantly felt like I was going to shatter or explode.

"Anyway," he said after a long silence. "I figure you need to find your thing. Hiking gave me something to focus on, something to do. I had to pay attention to keep myself safe and alive. It made me keep living even when I didn't want to."

"Do you still miss her?" I needed to know. I needed to know if the hollow darkness inside of me would ever lift.

"Every day. I always will. It gets easier though. The rawness of it all fades. The grief—despite what people will tell you—never goes away. Not really. It becomes part of you. Now I can look back on those five years and be happy and grateful. I was lucky. Blessed. I wish I'd had more years. An actual lifetime. I'm glad I got what I got. It's more than a lot of other people get."

He stood and reached out his hand to me. I took it, letting him pull me to my feet. I was grateful for him, for this moment he'd given me. My friends and family all tried to support me and take care of me and help me through this. Carson, though, had helped me more with a car ride and short conversation than anyone else ever had. Maybe it was because he was my age. Maybe it was because he, like me, hadn't had much time with his lost spouse. Maybe it was something else I couldn't ever put a name on. Whatever it was though, he'd given me hope, real hope, in my heart. Hope for better times, happier times, in my future.

Chapter Seven

Four days. Four days until what our paper was calling a "history-making trial." I wanted it all to go away. I wanted it over. I wanted to hide until it had passed. None of those things were going to happen though.

"Joy said you're not going to the trial."

Carson had just taken a seat at the counter and blurted out the statement. I'd been happy to see him. Until he opened his mouth and shined a spotlight on me. It wasn't lunch or dinner rush, but we were busy. Several people within earshot looked up when he spoke. They each looked away quickly, but they were still subtly leaning toward Carson. Mr. Murguia shook out his paper but stopped turning pages. Mrs. Worth studied her receipt with the dedication of a high school kid cramming for finals. Tommy Payne stopped watching Marisol with hearts in his eyes and pretended to look at the back of his cell phone. Rio Verde's two biggest gossips and the son of the third. I'd be mad at Carson but he didn't know the city gossip chain. I was still embarrassed at the sudden spotlight he had cast on me. Tommy's mom would be calling my mom before the hour was up. Mr. Murguia would have told the whole senior men's group at church by dinnertime. Mrs. Worth would probably hit the senior women's group and the quilting circle before she headed home for the day.

"You and Joy need to stop talking about me." Out of the corner of my eye, I saw Mr. Murguia quickly cover a laugh. "We're new friends and all but you need to talk directly to me instead of about me." My inner voice told me to rein it in, but he'd pushed a button. I was tired of everyone whispering about me. It had been a year, for Pete's sake. Everyone needed to stop acting like I was going to shatter at any moment.

Carson held up both hands, admitting defeat. "Whoa, whoa. A: I'm sorry. B: We weren't talking about you. She told me she was going to testify. I asked if you were testifying too. Then she told me you weren't even going to go to the trial."

I looked at him for a second, less irritated now. "Okay. We'll talk about this. In a minute."

I left Carson looking over a menu and went to clear out the gossips. "Mrs. Worth, are you ready to take care of your bill?" It was my turn to smother a laugh as the gray-haired, prim-and-proper lady jumped when I stopped at her table. "I'll meet you at the register. Didn't you say you had a hair appointment today?"

"No, no dear. A quilting circle meeting." She recovered her composure and gathered her purse and coat.

I detoured over to Tommy. I took his phone out of his hand, turned it the right way around, and whispered, "It works better this way." He flushed as red as his t-shirt when Marisol gave a little laugh. She beat me to Mr. Murguia.

"Mr. M., can I get you anything else? Some pie maybe? Or more coffee? It seems like you've got a lot of your paper left to read." He got flustered too, folding his paper and finishing his now-cold coffee. Quickly, each of them stood before the register. I checked them out, wishing them well, thrilled to have them out of the diner.

"Go take a break, sissy," Marisol said. "I'll watch over things."

"Thanks, Mari. Carson, come on. Help me clean up the kitchen."

Marisol swung open the gate, letting Carson behind the counter. He followed me into the kitchen then stopped, not sure what he was supposed to do now.

"Here," I said, tossing him a rag. "Clean anything that isn't used to cook the food."

He went to work while I tidied up, putting away things we'd used during breakfast and anything else we wouldn't need again today.

"So you're not going," he finally asked.

"No. One of the lawyers, one of the prosecutors, wanted me to be there. To cry on command or something. I'm not going to do that for them."

"I don't blame you there."

We worked without speaking for a while. I wondered what he thought of me, refusing to attend the trial of my husband's murderer. I wasn't really even sure what I thought of myself. I didn't want to go though. I didn't want to see crime scene photos or hear eyewitness testimony. I didn't want any of those details in my head. Mateo was gone. Nothing in that spectacle of the trial was going to bring him back. I wished the whole thing would just go away. That it would stop appearing everywhere. On the radio. On the news. In the paper. I wished the phone calls asking me for comments would stop.

"Do you feel like you owe it to him, to your husband, to be there? I feel like I would if I were in your shoes."

I turned to him, setting down the stack of empty crates I'd been about to take into the storeroom.

"I don't owe Teo that. I owe it to him to raise our daughter well. To make sure she never forgets him and always knows how much he loved her. To make sure he stays alive for her on some level. I don't owe it to him to give any of my attention to the man who took his life."

I was angry as I finished my little speech. Not angry at Carson for his question. Angry at the stupid, cowardly man who pointed a gun at a woman and child. He'd given Teo no choice because of the kind of man Teo was. Because he'd been high and scared and stupid he'd pointed a gun and my husband had shielded his intended victims. Because Teo had always taken care of other people first, he'd died. And I was angry. I was angry about every tiny moment, every random person, and even every single thing that had come together into the perfect storm that had ruined my world.

I grabbed the empty crates and stomped out of the room, quickly returning to finish up. I wanted out of there suddenly. I wanted to pack up Ria and go to a park or for a walk. I needed fresh air and activity to burn the anger out of me. Instead, I scraped the grill clean and did the rest of my work.

"I still think you should keep track of how the trial goes."

"Fine. That's your new job. You can follow it and give me a recap every evening."

Carson grinned but didn't say a word, probably trying to keep me from giving another angry speech. Instead, he worked side by side with me, not complaining about being roped into doing chores, not bringing up the trial again. My anger quickly cooled around his quiet peacefulness. It made me like him more. He knew when to back off. He also seemed to understand all the churning emotions inside of me. Probably better than anyone else could.

Chapter Eight

"I don't want to hear it." I slapped my hand over my mouth the second the words flew out. I couldn't believe I had said something like that to my preacher. "I'm so sorry, Dr. Bell. I don't know what came over me."

"Believe me, Luz, people have said worse things to me."

"I really am sorry. You had this look on your face as you walked up. This look that everyone seems to get when they see me alone. It said you were going to tell me something like you've been praying for me and one day things will be better. I'm tired of people telling me stuff like that. It doesn't help a stinking bit."

Dr. Bell smiled his understanding-preacher smile and gave me a one-armed hug.

"I'm sorry. You'll have to forgive all of us. We are all at a loss when it comes to helping someone as young as you move forward from such an awful loss. We're learning."

"So am I, sir. So am I." The music started to play in the sanctuary and we both rushed into the darkened room as the doors were being closed. He headed to the sound booth where he'd watch the worship part and prep for his sermon. I hurried down to the rows up front where my family was waiting. Mallie shoved Tres over when I appeared, freeing up the end seat for me.

"Why are you late?" She stopped singing and leaned over waiting for me to answer.

"Your uncle cornered me and I accidentally snapped at him. I feel awful."

"Don't. People yell at Uncle Noah all the time. You're probably the least mean person this week."

"Y'all be quiet." Will stuck his head between us, giving us both a good glare before leaning back to his seat behind us. Mallie rolled her eyes and resumed singing.

I tried to focus on the music. I even sang along but, like every Sunday since Teo had died, the music did nothing for me. Once it had lifted my heart up to Heaven. In the past, I'd known all the songs by heart and had sung with my eyes closed as I put my everything into singing praises. Now there was nothing. It was still beautiful music. I still found some enjoyment in the singing. The power I'd once found in praising and worshipping had gone away. I missed it but didn't know how to get it back. As we moved through song after song, I watched the people around me as they worshipped. Some sang with hands raised toward the sky. Others swayed and danced to the music. Some took it painfully serious and worshipped with a rigid sort of praise. They all had a peaceful happiness about them though. When the music ended and the sermon began I felt the same sort of disconnect. I didn't even want to be there. I wanted to skip church until whatever was broken in me was healed. With my two best friends though—Mallie, the preacher's niece, and Joy, his daughter-in-law—skipping church wasn't something I was able to get away with.

So I went. Sunday after Sunday. At first, everything would fade into a blur of noise. I didn't have to work to tune the music and the message out. I was too fried by grief and exhaustion to register anything for months and months. Now, over a year later, I had to work to not hear everything. I had to work to keep up the wall between me and my faith. I was still too angry and too confused to let God back into my life. I didn't understand how God could let such a terrible man live on when he had done so many terrible things. Now, each Sunday, that's what I focused on. My own anger and frustration. It was the only way I could keep Dr. Bell's voice out of my head. It was the only way I could keep from hearing the lessons he gave us each week. It had been working until today, until Dr. Bell got to the end of his sermon and started talking about the water pots.

40

"Now you all know the story about the man with two water pots. One had a crack in it and even though it leaked water, he didn't repair it. He instead let it water the path to the well, eventually causing the path to be bordered by flowers. It's a story told over and over to show how God can use even the most broken person." Dr. Bell paused and, I thought, gave me a quick look. "God can not only use our brokenness, but he can also create victory with it. In healing us, He can demonstrate His power and grace. Your healing, your growth, can be His victory. Think about this as you go about your week."

He stepped off the stage, leading the church in prayer as the praise team resumed their spots for the last bit of worship music. I didn't bow my head. Instead, I watched everyone around me pray as I turned over those final words.

Victory through brokenness.

Healing into victory and grace.

It was something I'd been told all my life in a thousand different ways. Something about the way Dr. Bell had packaged it today made the concept resonate differently.

If God can take brokenness and heal it, transforming it into something as beautiful as a victory in His name, I had hope. Maybe He could heal me with his grace. Maybe I could stop feeling so broken inside. I looked down when the idea stampeded into my head. Hope. *Maybe God hadn't left me alone with my grief after all.*

As the praise team started to sing, I thought back over all the lonely nights I'd reached out for Teo in my sleep, jarring awake when I found him gone. The times I'd spotted someone from behind who looked like him and had rushed away before I could think that he was still alive somehow. The tears and rage and grief and aching emptiness that had made me think I was all alone. I wondered if I'd been as alone as I'd thought. Suddenly it didn't seem as though I had been.

Chapter Nine

As was our tradition, we gathered for lunch after church. Tres, Mallie, Joy, Will, Isabel, Lane, Marisol, and me. Now Carson too. The core of us, Mallie and my siblings and myself and Will, had grown up in the tradition. Our parents had always had a family lunch after church. Rotating houses each Sunday until they started having it in the closed diner where all of us kids could run and play without any breakables nearby. We'd split up now. The senior members of the clan had a quiet lunch, usually at Mallie's dad's house. We younger generation had something more boisterous. Today the guys were arguing about high school sports.

We'd left them upstairs and headed down to the bakery, led by Mallie on her crutches. After several surgeries she'd become a pro on the stairs, charging up and down them faster than any of us could on two good legs. Ria loved the show so Mallie climbed the stairs a few times just to make her laugh.

After Ria got bored with Mallie we followed Joy into the kitchen. She often used Sunday lunch as a chance to test out new recipes and we were always willing to taste test for her. When she'd been making Mallie's wedding cake I tasted dozens of variations of the cake and the icing before Will had finally picked the winning combination and settled her indecision. Today it was cookies. She and Lane were trying out new recipes for fall- themed cookies. Pumpkin. Snickerdoodle. Oatmeal with cinnamon. We sat in the empty bakery and feasted on sugar until one by one the guys found us and joined in.

As soon as we had all reconvened in the same spot, I had to slip away. I had a sleeping toddler draped over me who had doubled in weight as she'd fallen asleep.

"Joy, can I borrow a bed before she becomes too heavy to move?" She nodded, unable to speak over a mouthful of pumpkin cookie. Before I could heft Ria onto my shoulder Carson stood, taking her without a word. I started to protest but she snuggled against him with a sleepy smile. I couldn't snatch her away from him if he got an instant smile like that. Plus something about the picture the two of them made…it tugged at my heart. I followed him through the back hallway and upstairs to the apartment. I led the way to the smallest bedroom. Joy always let me borrow it when Ria was in need of a nap. With Carson's help, I tucked her in, never waking her up.

"She's beautiful," Carson said, watching her sleep from the doorway.

I pushed a lock of dark hair off her forehead, giving her a kiss before I stood. "She's something else. Angel. Monster. Everything in between. I love her best sleeping though."

He chuckled. "She doesn't seem so bad when she's awake."

"No, that's not why. When she's sleeping I can still see her as a tiny baby. Every day with her is a gift but those tiny baby days were special. Watching her discover the world. She'd marvel at the smallest, most ordinary things. Once, for several days, she thought pulling tissues out of the box was the funniest thing ever. I emptied every box in the house just to get her to laugh." I suddenly realized I was describing the sort of moment Carson had never gotten to have with his son. I turned to him, not surprised to see a touch of sadness on his face.

"Oh Carson, I'm so sorry. I didn't think."

"It's okay. It was a good story. Maybe I'll still get my chance at making those kinds of memories one day."

"I bet you will. Now go back downstairs. Have some cookies. I'll stay up here with her for a while. Make sure she's totally out."

"Actually," he said as he walked away, disappearing into the other bedroom. He returned with a camera in his hand and a bag over his shoulder. The camera wasn't a little point-and-shoot like the one buried in the bottom of my purse. It was a professional camera. Big, black, sleek. It was intimidating. He carried it with an easy confidence I immediately admired. I'd have been terrified to drop it. "Would you mind if I snapped a couple of shots? She needs to be photographed."

I nodded, surprised by his request. No one had ever asked to photograph my kid. Or me. Or anyone I knew. At least no one who carried a fancy camera like a professional the way Carson did. I had snapshots from the wedding and lots of cell phone pictures of Ria but nothing formal or professional. Even Mallie and I hadn't hired pros for our weddings. Teo and I had been too broke and Mallie and Tres just hadn't thought about booking a photographer until the day of the wedding. We'd all made do with cell phones and point-and-shoot cameras in the hands of friends and guests. Only Joy had gotten a pro and that was only after her mom had insisted.

I watched from the doorway while he worked. Turning on a light then dimming it with a nearby t-shirt. Carefully adjusting the blanket over her. He stepped back, looked over the scene he'd created, and picked up the camera. He lifted it to his eye and transformed before me. The only thing I could think to compare it to was back when Mallie had still been dancing. The way she lost herself in ballet was so close to the way Carson disappeared into picture taking. I could have led a parade past the bedroom and he wouldn't have noticed. He only saw the world framed by his camera. It was fascinating to watch.

He snapped picture after picture, changing angles and lenses and the lighting until he stood up and stepped back. The spell was over. He was done. He was Carson again.

"I'll edit these tonight," he said, walking past me and stowing his stuff back in his room. "Ready to go back downstairs?"

"Can I see some of your pictures? I've only ever seen the one you took of Joy." I pictured the photo when I spoke. It hung in the bakery office in a small, simple frame, the photo no bigger than a sheet of paper. It packed an impact though, the simple photo in the simple frame. It looked like a stolen moment. Like something no one should have seen. Joy assured us all it was posed. A woman sitting under a blooming dogwood tree. Her bare back to the camera, her red hair

44

loose, bright against her fair skin. A tree, a field, and a woman. It was so simple and yet so breathtaking. I wanted to see more of his work. I hadn't realized how much I wanted to until he'd taken Ria's photos. I wanted to see what he saw through that camera. I wanted to see the world the way he did.

Carson smiled at me and disappeared back into the other bedroom, coming out with a laptop under his arm. He walked past me to the couch, then sat down and patted the seat beside him. I sat and he opened the laptop and set it half in my lap. He opened a program, clicked a few menu choices, and a slideshow of photos started to play. I watched in awe, making him stop the show to tell me about photos that really caught my attention. It was a whole different world shown through the lens of his camera.

"Hey y'all. What are you doing up here?" Will appeared behind us, Joy close behind.

"Oh, is Carson showing you pictures?"

Carson raised an eyebrow at Joy and she grimaced.

"I'm sorry. Is Carson showing you some of his . . . What's the right term?"

"Fine art photography," Carson supplied.

"Yes, is Carson showing you some of his Fine Art Photography?" I could hear the capital letters when Joy spoke. I smiled. She was enjoying teasing him.

"I'm holding her captive," Carson answered.

"Show her the ones from your last trip to Alaska. Will, you haven't seen them either."

Will joined us on the couch, sitting on the other side of Carson. After a couple of clicks, a different slide show started to play. A few photos in and both Will and I gasped. Carson stopped the show, grinning with pride. The photo was a stunner. A grizzly bear and two cubs. The mama bear sat on her haunches, content, watching her babies tumble and play in the grass before her.

"The bear?" Joy asked.

"Yeah," Carson answered.

45

"Where did you—" I started.

"How did you—" said Will.

"I took a friend backpacking in Denali National Park. We were out for seven days. Found this lady on the second day. I had to use my big zoom lens to get the shot, but it was worth it. We watched them for a couple of hours. Those cubs were amazing." He clicked a key on the computer and another photo appeared; this time it was the two cubs playing. One stood up on its hind legs while the other reached up with a paw. He clicked again, showing us photo after photo of the bears. When I finally left for the day we'd all made Carson promise to take us hiking in Alaska one day. Seeing his photos made all of us want to see the same wild world he'd captured in the photos. I wanted to disappear into that world for a while. I wanted to be able to capture the feeling of wonder and peace in those pictures and carry it with me all the time.

Chapter Ten

The magical peacefulness I'd left Joy's house with was gone the next day. Long gone. I broke three coffee cups and a plate during the breakfast rush. I was setting everything down too hard, with too much force. I couldn't keep orders straight. Took food to the wrong tables. It was like I'd never waited tables before. Dad finally made me come work in the kitchen, leaving Marisol and Mom to wait tables and help the customers. I couldn't get it together in there either, though. By lunchtime I was burning burgers and ruining fries. I made the coffee too strong and then too weak. I put too much sugar in the sweet tea. I broke more dishes, knocked over the mop bucket, and countless other things. I couldn't do anything right. I couldn't focus on anything.

At least not anything diner-related. What Carson had said the other night was haunting me, echoing in my head. *My thing. My thing to focus on. My version of hiking across the world.* It was the just about the only thought I could hold in my head.

It kept trading places with one other thought, though.

The Tate House.

As I cleaned up my fifth broken plate of the day, I realized something. The diner wasn't my thing. I wasn't working here because I was passionate about it. Mom. Dad. Marisol. They loved this place to a nearly irrational level. They happily sacrificed for the RWB over and over. I was here because I needed a job and knew working in the family business was expected of me.

Take the afternoon off, mija, Dad had finally said. From the side-eye glances everyone was giving me, each one a mix of sadness and pity, I knew that all three of them thought I was cracking up. I could tell Mari wanted to talk to me. She'd probably texted Isabel to tell her I was acting crazy. Shoot, she'd probably texted Grace too, as if she could do anything from all the way down at vet school. It was the sister text chain. I'd activated it myself many times. I had a best friend one, too, with Mallie and Joy. I didn't want to talk to any of them though. I took Dad's suggestion and split, gathering up Maria and getting out of there before anyone could try to talk to me. I went straight from the diner to the one place I knew I wouldn't run into any of my friends and family. My happy place.

The Rio Verde Library.

It was tucked away from the center of town near the Justice Center beside the original Rio Verde School. Though the city had outgrown the school years ago, the library hadn't changed locations in a hundred years. It was my favorite place in the whole town. Marisol loved our diner the most. Isabel, she loved the junk store on the edge of town. My big brother, the big farm and ranch store not far from his farm. Mallie, a hardware store the next town over. Every member of my family had their refuge. The library had always been mine. It was the only place I didn't feel the internal volcano of grief-rage welling up inside of me. It was a place that had been mine before Teo. It was a place that wasn't haunted by his ghost.

*****

"Why Luz Baca, is that you? What are you doing away from The Red, White, and Blue?"

The sudden question came from the tiny woman who had nearly crashed into me. Her voice was powerful and filled the quiet library with a burst of sound. No one hushed her though. No one hushed Patsy Tate. I'd just found the book I'd been hunting for and hadn't expected to run into anyone in the science fiction section, especially not her.

"It sure is, Miss Patsy. I'm taking a little break from the diner. Clearing my head."

Miss Patsy smiled at me—a kind, loving smile, not the poor-young-widow smile I had gotten used to receiving. I'd been trying to work up the nerve to go talk to her about the house, but she'd always been so intimidating to me. A tiny woman who was a force of nature. I was always surprised when she spoke to me, knew me by name. She never came to the diner and didn't go to our church, but she knew me. Miss Patsy knew everyone in Rio Verde.

"And where is that little one of yours?"

"Ruby stole her from me the second I walked in."

Ruby was the newest addition to the library staff. She was close to my own age and had been hired to start a children's reading program. Ria had taken to her right away. Normally, Ruby was busy with school kids needing help with homework but since we were here in the middle of the day, she was able to hang out with Ria, keeping her entertained while I hunted for a book or two for myself. I'd tried reading every book I had in the house. Nothing would hold my attention. Hopefully, something different from the library would help settle the unease inside of me and distract me from the approaching trial. I could escape the constant news it generated. Hide from it for a little while.

Miss Patsy blessed Ruby's heart, her voice finally dropping to what passed as a whisper for her. She then linked her arm with mine and guided me down the aisle of books to a pair of chairs sitting in front of one of the library's tall, wide windows.

"Let's sit and chat, dear." She claimed one chair and set down the stack of books she'd been carrying.

I took in her outfit in a quick glance as I claimed the other chair. Knee-high red boots right out of the 1970s. White jeans that were probably the same vintage. A baggy gold sweater she probably picked up at Goodwill. You'd never know she was the richest woman in town.

I settled in opposite her, holding the book I'd been carrying in my lap. I clung to it, unwilling to let it go. It was one Mateo had always told me to read. One he'd loved. *The funniest science fiction book ever*, he'd claimed. It had called to me, drawn me in today. I had to read it. I'd always promised to but never did. I was going to remedy that now.

"Luz, sweet girl, I've been watching you this past year." I didn't ask how she'd been watching. I'd learned that certain people in Rio Verde had eyes everywhere. Miss Patsy was one of those people. My mom said she always knew what went on in town, even if she hardly ever left her house.

"I think everyone has, ma'am."

She nodded. She'd lived here for every single one of her seventy plus years. She knew how this town was. Close-knit. Sometimes *too* close-knit. Sometimes you walked around with a spotlight on you.

"I'm sure they have. This town loves you, Luz. They loved your husband too. They've been grieving with you."

Grief rose up inside of me, hard and fast, choking me. I couldn't speak. I couldn't even look at her. If I did my control would have shattered.

"They grieved with me when I lost my Robbie. For the first few years after he passed, though, their support was suffocating. I imagine that's what you're feeling lately."

I nodded, still unable to speak around my strangling emotions. Suffocating was the right word. Every whispered conversation I'd overheard, every offer of help, every pity-filled glance—they were suffocating me. They had been since the moment Teo had died.

"I'm guessing you're also feeling stuck. Like you need to do something before you scream."

I nodded again, this time daring to look up at her. She'd honed right in on what was wrong like Carson had. All of my normal life stuff was wrong now without Mateo by my side. I needed to restart my life somehow.

"I thought so." She leaned closer to me, lowering her voice to a normal person's whisper. "That's why I wanted to talk to you. I think maybe I can help you."

Miss Patsy and I sat in the little nook by the windows until the library closed – early because it was Monday and the two main

50

librarians had choir practice on Mondays. Like the drive with Carson, talking with Patsy helped me more than any conversation with my well-meaning friends. Even my Tio Jonah hadn't helped as much. Maybe it was because Carson was the only person around my age that I knew who had faced this sort of a loss. Maybe it was because Patsy was another wife who had lost her husband. I didn't know. But talking with someone who had known such a similar grief, who had walked through it like I was now. They both offered me a level of support and solace that no one else could. Patsy told me of her husband's sudden heart attack and the aching, lonely grief that had swallowed her afterward. Her children had tried to help her but they each had families of their own to return to, lives to get on with. So Patsy had been left alone in the big house. Alone with her grief and the ghost of the life she'd once had. She'd wallowed and hid away for years. By the time our talk had ended, I knew she was trying to keep me from doing the same things she had. Trying to keep me from being consumed by my grief.

It was a sobering window to look into. I could wallow and let my grief swallow me, like Miss Patsy had. I could see myself heading down the same path. The anger. The empty, hollow feeling inside of me. They wanted to swallow me whole. I could feel it.

When we parted at the library doors, Ria back in her spot on my hip, I'd decided two things. I wasn't going to let this grief, this loss, define me. And somehow I was going to buy the Tate House. I wasn't just going to *try* to buy it. I was going to *get* it. I didn't know what I'd do with the house once it was mine but I'd figure it out.

Chapter Eleven

"Someone made me laugh the other day. A sort of friend. A new friend. Joy's friend Carson. It was the first time I'd laughed without you." I looked up from yellowed grass to the still-new headstone. *Mateo Luis Baca. Son. Friend. Husband. Father.* His parents had fought me on it. They'd wanted something more their taste: his photo on the stone and a Virgin Mary statue. Teo had left a will behind though—something that had surprised me. In it had been detailed instructions for his funeral and headstone. He seemed to have known that someday there might be a battle about those things. He had found a way to still take care of me even from Heaven.

I reached out to the stone, the icy cold seeping into my hand. The November sun hadn't warmed the air and wouldn't warm the stone much at all given how chilly it was today. Stupid cold front. I wanted the warmth of two days ago back. I ignored my frozen fingers and traced the words, running my fingertips over the sharp, clean letters of the epitaph. I felt guilty for having laughed with Carson and Joy, for having had a moment of normal happiness. I felt like I should still be weeping and wearing black and mourning.

"I don't know how to do this, Teo. I don't know how to mourn you and still live life. I don't know how to keep being Ria's mom and stop being your wife. How long am I supposed to be sad? Is there a list of guidelines somewhere? Rules I should follow?" I ran out of questions and let my voice trail off into the morning quiet. I should get up, get in my car, and get Ria out of the cold. I couldn't move though. I watched her for a second, playing on the crisp, pale yellow grass all bundled up in her warm coat and fuzzy blue hat. I wished I could be like her. For her, it was a normal day. Her brain wasn't old enough to understand what she'd lost. A big part of me was jealous of her lack of understanding. She asked where he was a lot but was always satisfied when I answered with *Heaven*.

"Why'd you have to do it? Why'd you have to step between a stranger and the shooter? Why'd you leave us?" I knew why he'd done it though. Because he was Mateo. Because he always took care of people. It was one of the big reasons I'd fallen in love with him. He had always had this protective drive. I could remember him as a kid, always shadowing my big brother. He'd balanced Tres' hot head. Done his best to keep him out of trouble. He and Tres had always had the same agenda but had approached it in very different ways. I thought of Tres, wondering how he had handled this loss so well. I knew if I'd lost a friend . . . if I'd lost my oldest and best friend, I'd be wrecked. In the year since we'd lost Teo, I'd hardly seen Tres. Church and lunch each Sunday and other group things but no one-on-one time. He'd been putting in long hours farming, cutting hay, loading it for customers. He had started clearing another area of the farm that had been overtaken by trees and weeds. He wanted to expand wherever he could so he could farm as much as possible. Between farming and taking care of Mallie after her two knee surgeries, he'd spent the last year covered up with work. I was sure it was how he was coping without his best friend. Filling the void Teo had left with work. I needed to go check on him, properly. Have a brother-sister conversation. I'd been so focused on getting Ria and myself through this that I hadn't worried about how he was getting through it.

I needed to go check on other people too I realized. Teo's parents. I'd barely seen them recently. I'd tried more with them than I had with Tres, done a bit better job I hoped. I'd taken them dinner once a week for months after, so they could spend time with Ria. They'd been as cool and distant to me at those dinners as they had been before everything fell apart. I would never be good enough for their son. Teo's sister Tia had only really warmed up to me after he'd passed. She would at least text me from time to time, but only to see how Maria was doing. They'd all thought I'd trapped him by getting pregnant. We had explained our elopement over and over, but it had

53

never sunk in with his parents. I would always be the girl who had trapped Teo and forced him into a job at a truck stop that had eventually gotten him killed. I couldn't win with them.

Our weekly dinners had finally stopped when they'd gone on a vacation in the spring. Then they had spent a long time with his sister and her husband over in Phoenix before resuming traveling around most of the summer. I wasn't even sure they were back in town. I should have reached out to them more even though I'd never been their favorite person. They'd lost their son. They were hurting as much as I was. Even more. Mom had told me burying your own child was a parent's worst fear. It was life out of order; parents should go first. I understood it. I wouldn't want to keep living myself if I lost Ria.

"I'll go check on your folks soon, I promise." I reached out, laying my hand over his name. I pretended, for a few seconds, that I was instead laying my hand over his heart. I'd done it so many times when he was alive. I could almost feel his heart thudding against my palm.

"I miss you." I shifted again, getting more comfortable as I settled in to talk to him a bit longer. "I got a check from your life insurance company a while ago. You're still surprising me. I never knew you'd thought of all of these things. Your will. A college fund for Ria. Now this." I paused, thinking back. We'd agreed to split up all the adult-stuff, as he'd called it, when we married. He was great with numbers and money, so he took charge of our finances. I handled the car insurance and the house. We'd taken turns on other stuff like grocery shopping and keeping up the house. I was still struggling to handle it all by myself.

"It's a lot of money, Teo. I think I'm going to try to use it to buy the Tate House if I can. That big old house is probably priced way above what I can afford but I feel like I have to at least try. It went up for sale a few days ago. Remember that one time we talked about having our own little inn? It'd be the perfect house for it, don't you think?"

54

Silence was my answer. The wind came up and swept a scattering of leaves toward Ria and me. They stopped short though, not blowing into us but instead coming to rest before Ria's blanket, the momentum of the wind making them shiver and shudder for a second before they stilled. She squealed in joy and reached out to gather the leaves, smiling as she crushed them then threw the pieces in the air. I wondered if the little gust of wind was Teo's way of saying he liked my idea. I chose to believe it was.

I touched his name one more time as I pushed myself up, lifting my hand away from the gravestone only when I was standing. I glanced around the cemetery. Not another person was in sight. It was peaceful. A good start to a new day. A new day which would hopefully change a lot of things in my life. *In our life*, I corrected as I gathered up Maria and her blanket.

Chapter Twelve

I stared at the bank slip in my hand. I'd asked the teller for the balance of our bank accounts. My bank accounts. It was in there. The check from Teo's life insurance had gone through. It was real money. More money than I'd make in twenty years working at the diner. The life insurance policy had been dated before we'd even started going out. The lawyer from Mr. Coulter's office had told me Teo'd changed it, adding me as the sole beneficiary after our second date. If he were still alive I'd give him crap about jumping the gun on our relationship. I might still give him crap about it the next time I went to the cemetery.

"Can you check it one more time?" The teller smiled and punched a couple of keys on her computer, handing me the slip when it printed. It was identical to the first one.

"Good news," she asked.

"The first in a long time," I said, tucking the slips into my pocket. I told her thank you and picked up Ria, heading to my third stop for the day.

*****

"Oh! You're back two days in a row!"

Ruby. Bless her heart. I smiled as she hurried across the empty library toward me. She wasn't the typical librarian. No dresses. No cardigans. She did wear glasses but everything about her was different from the stereotypical librarian. She was almost always in jeans and flip-flops, even now as winter approached. She always sported book related t-shirts too, something that seemed to amuse all the kids. Ruby was more grown-up kid than serious librarian and I loved her for it.

"I needed another day off from the diner."

"I'm not going to complain. Need me to keep an eye on my favorite kiddo for a bit?"

"You don't mind? I need to borrow a computer for a while."

Ruby nodded and reached out her arms so I passed over Ria and her bag of stuff. I reminded myself to bring over some goodies for Ruby. She'd been so helpful since she'd come to town, watching Ria for me every single time I came to the library. I needed to make her dinner or something.

Once I had a computer in front of me I got to work. First I found the real estate listing for the Tate House, printing out the flyer with the contact information for the realtor. There wasn't a price listed for the house. It simply said all offers on the house would be considered on a case-by-case basis by Mrs. Tate personally. I wondered what that meant.

Next, I hit Google, searching for information on small inns and bed and breakfasts. I printed out several articles to read later. After another search, I found and printed out the local rules for turning a residence into a business. The last thing I printed was a list of contacts at the county offices. I knew I'd need those if I were able to make this crazy idea happen. I stared at the computer for a bit, trying to think of anything else I might need to print out. I hated not having a computer at home but it was a cost Teo and I hadn't been able to justify. Then I remembered the slips in my pocket from the bank.

"I guess now I could swing it," I said to myself, pulling up Amazon and searching for laptops. For a half hour, I switched between Amazon and review sites until I'd picked out a laptop. I put in Joy's address at the bakery instead of mine for the ship-to. There was someone there all day. She could sign for it and keep it for me. I thought about having it sent to the diner but I didn't think Mom and Dad would be very supportive of my plan so I went with Joy instead.

"Okay, so you're the reason I keep hearing a printer go off."

I jumped out of my skin at the sudden voice right behind me. I'd been so focused on the computer I hadn't even heard anyone walk up, let alone noticed Carson's familiar face.

"Oh geez, you scared the fire out of me."

A hidden person whisper-shouted *shhhhhh* at us and we both flushed.

"Sorry," Carson said. "I was reading right over there," he paused and pointed to a lone chair beside a nearby window, "and I kept hearing a printer fire up. I finally had to see who was working so hard over here."

"Yeah. It's me." I stepped around him, crossing the little computer area to the printer. From the raised platform, I could see most of the library's first floor. There were more people browsing around than when I'd first gotten here. "What time is it?"

Carson checked his watch and announced that it was lunchtime.

"Shoot. I left Ria with Ruby way too long." I hurried to stack my papers and gather my stuff but Carson stopped me, taking the printed pages from me and flipping through them.

"Interesting reading."

"Thanks, Nosey," I said, snatching them out of his hands. He grinned at me and I felt myself flush.

"I think we should go have lunch and talk."

"Oh really? Why?"

He held up the book I hadn't noticed him set on the table next to a computer. A book about starting a small business. I studied him a second, surprised that a near-stranger was thinking along the same lines I was. I wondered what he was planning.

"Hmm. You might be right," I finally said. "Maybe we do need to go have lunch and talk."

I took Carson to Dot's BBQ for lunch. I was surprised to learn Joy and Will hadn't taken him yet. We ate and talked and took turns picking up the things Ria tossed to the floor from her high chair. As it turned out, Carson had been thinking about the Tate House too.

"I grew up in a bed and breakfast," he told me as he picked at the plate of French fries we'd been sharing. "Weird, funky place. Each room had a theme. My mom was always redoing them, re-theming them."

"That must have been fun. More fun than growing up in a diner."

"Yeah. It really wasn't," Carson said, making me smile. "There were a lot of clogged toilets. Lots of people eating too much gumbo and drinking too many Hurricanes. I've cleaned up way too much puke."

"You may win. I've unclogged my fair share of toilets at the diner though. Not much puke. Lots of little kid birthday parties though. They're an unholy mess."

For over an hour, he told me about growing up in the heart of New Orleans. He'd always run from the family business, he explained. Tried to make his own way in the world. Ever since he'd seen the for sale sign in front of the Tate House, the idea of following in his mother's footsteps didn't seem so bad anymore. I could have kept talking to him for hours. He was funny and his stories about his mom's bed and breakfast made me excited about having one of my own someday.

Dot herself finally came out and chased us off, ordering us to stop hogging the table, then gave us both a slice of apple pie to take home. By the time I dropped Carson back off at the library, we had the start of a plan. A plan I was excited about. Excited for the first time in way too long.

Chapter Thirteen

"So I talked to my mom last night. About our idea. She gave me a list of things we need to do if we're going to turn the Tate House into a B and B."

Carson didn't say hello. Just charged into the diner and sat down at the counter right across from me. With anyone else, it would have been annoying but with him, it was sort of endearing.

I carefully set an empty coffee cup in front of him. Dad had let me come back to work on probation. If I broke anything I was forever banished to the office and the accounting ledgers and the supply orders. I hadn't told him about the Tate House plan. Given how poor a worker I'd been lately, I kind of thought he'd be okay with me quitting, but I didn't want him to find out by overhearing my potential business partner flapping his big mouth.

"Shush. My dad doesn't know anything about this. I don't want him to find out about it from you."

"Sorry," he said, a look on his face that was nearly a mirror image of Tres' dog Trouble when he'd gotten yelled at. Sheepish and sorry. A scolded puppy.

"It's okay. Coffee?"

He shook his head no and instead pulled out a little leather-bound notebook from his jacket pocket. "Can we plan?"

I looked away from him, scanning the diner. It was mostly empty. The daily lull between breakfast and lunch. Marisol was back in the office doing homework for her college classes. Dad was in the kitchen cleaning up the breakfast mess. Mom had just left with Ria to run a few errands. It was the best time we'd get all day.

"Are you serious about this? Going into business? With me? Staying in Rio Verde?"

Carson narrowed his eyes and thought for a second. I could almost see the wheels turning in his head as he quickly made a decision.

"Yeah, I am. This feels right."

"Okay, then, let's plan," I said, putting away the coffee and mug before giving him my full attention. "What'd your mom say?"

He opened the notebook and started reading off a list. It was all great things that would have taken me months of research to come up with. Zoning laws. Business licensing. Legal contracts. Health codes. Marketing. Budgets. I wanted to hug the woman. She was going to be a wealth of information I could already tell. I wanted to go over his quickly-read list but I was sure someone in my family would bust us before we could get everything ironed out. Right now, it was just an idea we had. I didn't want them to find out until it was a reality.

"Your mom is kinda my favorite person right now."

"Right? Mine too. She's excited for us to do this. Thinks it'll be great."

"Who thinks what will be great," my dad asked, appearing behind me.

"Umm . . ."

"Carson's mom thinks it will be great if Carson . . ."

"If I decide to stay here permanently." An obvious, hurried lie but my dad didn't call him out on it. Instead, he handed me his apron and shook his car keys.

"I've got to run a quick errand. Hold down the fort. Feed people. That sort of stuff. Make Carson help you."

"I'd be happy to help out, sir."

Hearing Carson call my dad *sir* cracked me up for some reason. It was so out of character for him. Despite being from the south, he hadn't struck me as a *sir* or *ma'am* kind of guy. I held my laughter in check until my dad walked out the front door.

"What? What'd I say?"

61

"Just," I gasped, catching my breath. "Just hearing you call him sir. You suddenly became a proper Southern gentleman. It was just a bizarre transformation."

He smiled and gave a little chuckle. "It was even more bizarre on my side of it. I was suddenly a sixteen-year-old guy in front of the father of a girl he likes. It was so strange. My mom would be so proud to know I've still got the manners she worked so hard to teach me."

A girl he likes. My mind skipped everything he'd said and held onto those words for a second. I pushed them away quickly. *They didn't mean anything* I said to myself. It didn't matter anyway. We were friends. Possible business partners. Nothing more.

"Anyway, now he's gone, let's look up the zoning for the Tate House." I pulled my cell phone out, pulling up Google and starting to search. Carson set his list on the counter and pulled out his phone.

"I'll look up the health code laws for bed and breakfast in Texas."

Carson pulled out his phone and started to search, and even though I preferred a real computer, I followed his lead. Together we added notes to the list until my dad's car appeared in front of the diner again.

"Dad's back. You keep researching," I said, stowing my phone and sliding his notebook back to him. "Not here though. He'll get suspicious."

He acted quickly, putting away his own phone and his notebook, slipping off the stool as my dad walked in.

"Okay, Luz, now that your dad is back I'm out of here. Got to find a place to live since I'm staying." He sir-ed my dad again as he walked out. I watched him through the window, giggling at his bright red face.

The rest of the day Dad kept giving me weird looks. They were the sort of looks he'd given Mallie and me when we'd been plotting some sort of mischief. We'd usually been planning to go swim in a pool belonging to someone out of town, foolishness that landed us in the back of a police car a few times. I knew he was suspicious.

Hopefully, he wouldn't start digging. There wasn't really anything to find. Just notes in Carson's notebook. Articles printed out at my house. Ideas in our heads. I told myself I wasn't hiding anything from him. I wasn't lying or sneaking. I was exploring an idea, nothing more.

Chapter Fourteen

They were having so much fun. The impromptu dinner, a happy, unplanned gathering. First Mallie and Tres had stopped by at closing. Then Joy and Will had walked over from the bakery. Then Carson had reappeared. Joy had called Lane. I'd called Isabel. Tres and I had cooked burgers and fries for everyone, sending Dad home and promising to clean up and lock up when we were done. I loved it when things fell into place so perfectly.

I watched them all, laughing, talking over each other. Happy. I stood in the empty and mostly dark diner and watched for a second longer, the iced tea I'd gone to get forgotten in my hand. My friends. My family. Tres and Mallie. Joy and Will. Isabel. Lane. Now Carson. Maria sat in Tres' lap, sound asleep and leaning back against him. Once we'd all fit into the big corner booth, back when it had been Mallie, Tres, Teo, and me. Our group had grown and now we had to spread out onto a second table. My people. I loved them. All that was missing was Mateo.

The second he popped into my head a memory blindsided me. I looked over to the front door and saw him as he'd looked the day he'd moved back to Rio Verde. I hadn't seen him in years, not since he and Tres had graduated from high school. He'd headed off to a mechanical school down by Dallas right after graduation. Teo had walked into the diner one afternoon out of the blue. Older. A little taller. With a new short haircut and a pair of aviator sunglasses. He was a new man. I was gone in a second. A voice in my head instantly whispered *I'm going to marry that man.* I learned later, after we'd started dating, that the same thought had been in his head when he'd seen me. Meant to be. It's what he'd said we were. Meant to be.

64

"Hey, sis! You get lost?" Tres pulled me back to the present. "I'm dying of thirst over here."

"No, you're not. You still have tea in your glass." I sat the pitcher in front of him and he grinned and filled his glass then passed the tea on. It made the rounds and was quickly emptied. I should have grabbed two, I thought as I reclaimed my chair beside Mallie.

"Where'd you go?" She whispered the question in my ear, bumping my shoulder with hers as she leaned over.

"To get tea."

"You know what I mean."

"Yeah. I do. Just remembering for a sec."

She didn't answer, only leaned against me for a second. I looked up from the remnants of my burger and fries and caught Carson watching me from across the table. I knew he'd caught the exchange and I knew he'd understood where I'd gone.

It was Carson's second dinner with everyone. He'd fit in instantly. Even though his past visits had been a day or two with Joy, she had told us all about him so we all felt as if we'd become friends with him long ago. He'd stood up to teasing from Tres and Joy. He'd stood up to Will's prying questions. Lane and Isabel had simply accepted him, welcoming him in right away. Mallie had welcomed him in quickly too, accepting him, happy to see Joy happy.

"Y'all, I think I'm going to buy the Tate House. Turn it into a bed and breakfast. Anyone want to go in on it with me?" I didn't know where the words had come from. They'd charged right past the part of my brain that filtered my thoughts and headed right out of my mouth. Everyone went silent and turned to stare at me.

"The Tate House. The big house down the road?" It was Carson who asked, pretending he didn't know. We hadn't talked about telling everyone our plan but he was following my lead, quickly picking up on my impulse.

"Yup."

"That is a really cool house."

"I know."

"Do you know anything about running a B and B?"

"Nope. Stayed in one for my honeymoon. That's it."

"I grew up in one. My mom still runs it down in New Orleans."

He said it like a native. *N'awlins.* It was the most obvious his accent had ever been. For someone who had grown up with only Texas accents in her ears, it was novel and fun.

"Really?" It was Mallie who asked. I dared to glance over at her and could see her wheels were turning. For a former ballet dancer, she had a head for business like no one else.

"Yup."

She looked to Joy for confirmation.

"He did. Right in the French Quarter. I've been there. Super cool place."

Mallie locked back on Carson, studying him with narrowed eyes.

I watched him too, staring him down for a second. Then I remembered something Miss Patsy had said to me. *You need to do something new. Something that belongs to you, not to you and your dead husband.* She'd said it took her nearly five years to figure it out. I'll be damned if it was going to take me so long. I was going to take the idea Carson and I had talked about and make it real.

"Wanna stick around Rio Verde? Go into business with me?"

I heard Mallie whisper my name under her breath and glanced over at my best friend. On her face was a question. Several in fact. She thought I was crazy. She wanted to know if I was sure. She wanted to know all the details. If I had a plan. How I was going to pay for everything. I knew her. She probably already had a list started in her head. I nodded at her and turned back to Carson again.

He was watching me. I didn't know him well enough yet to read him. I had a feeling he liked a challenge though. I had a feeling this would be a good gamble—going into business with him.

"Hell yes, I do." He stood and thrust his hand across the table toward me. I stood too, reaching out and grabbing his hand, sealing the deal.

"I can't believe you just did that," Mallie whispered.

"Damn, sis," Tres chimed in.

Soon everyone was talking again, talking over each other, asking questions and not waiting for answers. It was the most . . . alive our group, our tribe, had been since Teo had been killed. I could feel him there, in the noise. Hovering on the edges of everything. Happy.

Chapter Fifteen

I stood side by side with Carson on the sidewalk in front of the Tate House. There was a faint coat of frost on everything—trees, buildings—they all wore a glittering coat of white. Both of us kept exhaling clouds of steam as we talked about our plan. The cold would vanish as the sun rose and chased away this last cold front but I wasn't thinking about that. I was barely focused on my conversation with Carson. I kept getting distracted by my own excitement. Childhood dreams of living in the big, fancy house kept flooding my brain.

"A little excited?" Carson asked.

"So excited." I bounced on my toes a few times, giving release to some of my pent-up glee. "I haven't been this pumped about something since . . ." I paused and searched my brain. "Since the doctor told me I was having a girl."

Carson started to say something but the arrival of another car silenced him. It was the realtor. My heart skipped a beat and I felt like a kid who had found out the biggest present under the Christmas tree had their name on it. I looked over at Carson and for the first time, he looked as excited as I was.

"Mr. and Mrs. Baca?" the realtor asked as she approached. She was tiny and blonde and impressively cheerful for so early in the morning.

"No," Carson corrected. "I'm Carson LeBlanc and this is Luz Baca. We're business partners."

"Oh, I'm sorry. When you called and made the appointment, Mrs. Baca, I just assumed I'd be meeting with a family."

"It's no big deal," I assured her as I shook her hand. She must be from out of town, I thought to myself. Someone local would have registered my last name and started talking about my loss or my brave husband or the trial starting today. *Nope. Not thinking about that.* I'd been telling myself that all morning. The trial had been the main topic on all the local TV and radio stations. It was hard to not think about something when you were practically being force-fed news about it.

"Let's start the tour, shall we?" She trotted past us on her sky-high heels, tap-tap-tapping her way up the long sidewalk to the front door. She unlocked the front door and gestured for us to come inside. "As you can see, the Tate House is a stunning example of Victorian Gothic architecture. It's been mostly untouched inside, aside from the addition of modern wiring and plumbing. A central heating and cooling system was also added but not in a way which detracts from the original style of the home." She tapped her way down the main hallway, rattling off more and more information on the home. I hoped Carson was paying attention because I was tuning her out as I lagged behind, taking in each room slowly.

It was dark. That was my first reaction. The wood trim and paneling in each room bore a dark stain. The floors were maybe one shade lighter. They were all covered up by heavy, jewel-toned rugs so it was hard to know their true color. The windows were all covered by heavy brocade curtains in shades of gold and red. Even with lights on in each room, everything was still dark and gloomy.

My second thought was that there was so much wallpaper. Every hallway was wallpapered from the wainscoting to the ceiling. Through tunnels of dark wood and wallpaper we followed the realtor—Sandie, with an I and an E, she'd informed us. The heavy patterned, dark colored paper was going to be stamped on my brain forever. It was overwhelming and the first thing I'd get rid of after we bought the house. The very first thing.

Maybe the second thing, I thought, when Sandie cheerily informed us most of the furnishings and decor items would be sold with the house. With those words ringing in my head I got overwhelmed again. The rooms were stuffed with furniture. Over half of it could be sold and there would still be plenty of places to sit. The

69

walls all bore framed artwork and every flat surface held vases, figurines, and other stuff. So. Much. Stuff.

I made a mental list of the rooms on the first floor as we climbed the wide staircase to the second floor. Dining room. Living room. Den. Library. Study. Kitchen. A bedroom and bathroom off the kitchen for household staff. There was a lot of space to de-clutter and de-wallpaper.

The second floor proved to be less of a potential project. Six big bedrooms, each with a bathroom. A sitting room in the tower on the front of the house. Wallpaper in the hallway, of course, but the rooms weren't too cluttered and were free of the heavy, dark curtains that clad all the windows on the first floor. All of the rooms save one had an abandoned feel to them. Dust had collected on all the flat surfaces and the neatly made beds looked as though they'd been untouched for years. The room Miss Patsy clearly still lived in was a cluttered mess. Pill bottles on the dresser. A stack of library books on one of the nightstands. A laundry basket of clothes in a chair. Stacks of newspapers and magazines on the floor. I thought of the woman I'd visited with at the library. She didn't match with the sad, old lady who lived in this room.

I followed Sandie and Carson back to the first floor, thinking hard about the house as a whole. It was a house full of ghosts. Ghosts of ancestors long gone. Ghosts of children now grown and gone. Ghosts of full lives lived then whittled down into sad, lonely endings. Ghosts everywhere but none of them were mine.

I wanted the house even more now. I wanted to exorcise those ghosts and make it a happy place again. I needed to.

"So what do you think? Don't you just love the house?"

Carson and I looked at each other. We didn't need to say anything. I could see on his face and knew he could see on mine—we both loved the house and wanted it very much.

"We're very interested in buying it," I said.

Sandie squealed like a little kid and clapped her hands. "Oh, that's just wonderful! Let me make a phone call and we'll go on to the next step." She turned and tapped away from us, pulling out her phone and disappearing into the library.

"Next step?" Carson looked confused as he watched her walk off.

"No idea. I thought she'd give us a price and we could go figure stuff out at the bank."

"Right? Me too."

We both looked toward the room Sandie had disappeared into then looked at each other.

"I love this house, don't you?" Carson said.

"I love it so much," I answered. "It's just . . ."

"There is a crap-ton of wallpaper."

"Yes! And so much other stuff."

"We can sell most of it."

"Or donate it to a museum."

Carson nodded and looked down the hallway again. I knew what he was thinking. I was thinking it too.

"We're going to be stripping wallpaper for months," I said, making him laugh.

We both froze when Sandie appeared again. I didn't breathe as she tapped down the hallway toward us.

"Okay, then. We're all set." She paused, looking from Carson to me, grinning.

"Set for what?" Cason asked.

"The next phase," she said, so enthusiastically that I expected her to clap again or give a little hip-hip-hooray cheer. "If you're both free for a bit longer, we'll meet with Mrs. Tate now. She's requested to sit down with all potential buyers to discuss their plans for the property. We'll walk over to the guest house. You need to see it too, after all."

She turned and tapped her way down the hall on her silly heels, leaving Carson and me no choice but to follow her. Back through the house we went, to the kitchen then out into the backyard. Across the small flower garden stood a small house with a single car garage. It was the same orange-red brick as the main house, with the same white trim and a steeply pitched roof. It didn't look as old but looked as though it was built to match the big house. Surrounded by the flower garden with ivy climbing the walls and arching over the windows, it looked a bit like a fairytale cottage. A winding gravel path connected it to the main house. Down this path Sandie headed, struggling a bit in the gravel on her stilettos. Carson and I both stopped, looking around the backyard. Even with the color seeped out of everything by the fall chill, it was beautiful. Beyond the flower garden was a wide green lawn anchored at the far end by a big gazebo. With a little work, we could turn it backyard into a peaceful oasis for guests. I could probably even get Tres to help me put in a vegetable garden. Maybe a few fruit trees too. I wondered if Carson was thinking along the same lines.

Sandie cleared her throat and got our attention. We refocused and headed toward her. When we got close, she opened the door to the guest house and walked inside, again leaving us no choice but to follow. We entered through the kitchen and followed Sandie to the living room on the other side. I stopped hard when I saw Miss Patsy sitting in a chair, open book in her lap, smile on her face.

"Luz, dear, sit down, please, and introduce your friend. We've got a lot to talk about."

Chapter Sixteen

I woke early the next day. For a few seconds, I was excited. Everything from the day before rushed back in. The tour of the Tate House. Talking with Miss Patsy and telling her about our plan for the house. She'd been intrigued by the idea. After our conversation, Sandie ushered us out of the guest house and finally told us the reason for the meeting with Miss Patsy. Turns out she didn't want to simply sell the house. She wanted it to go to someone who would love and treasure it the way all of her family had done. Generations of Tates had treated the house as more than a home—as a member of the family. She wanted to make sure the next owners would too. I was worried our idea to turn it into a business wouldn't meet her criteria.

But I was hopeful.

Hopeful. I hadn't used the word much since Mateo died. Now the feeling was seeping back into my life. *Hope.* I guessed it was a good thing, being hopeful. I was looking forward. Looking toward the future. Looking toward a life without Teo. A life without the missing-him-grief I'd been carrying around. I guess everyone was right. You did start to heal. Things did start to get easier.

My phone dinged and I reached for it, tugging it free from the charging cable to read the text.

"Crap," I whispered as I read the message from my brother. *Day two. You coming?* Four words and my hopefulness crashed down and my excitement tumbled after it.

The trial. I'd been able to keep it pushed out of my head yesterday. The rush from touring the Tate House had been that strong, had lasted all day. Tres brought it all back though, pushed the joy aside. The man who'd ruined my world was going to answer for his actions. I should have been excited about it just like I was excited about the possibility of the Tate House. I was dreading it instead. Dreading what might happen. The truth was I was scared.

What if the jury didn't find him guilty?

What if he went free?

What if he killed someone else?

I was so scared all of those things would happen. I was scared of all the other things could happen that I hadn't even though of yet. I looked down at the phone again, clearing the notification. I thought for a moment then bowed my head. *Please, Lord, make sure that man never hurts anyone again.* I prayed like I hadn't prayed in months. I prayed until I heard Maria wake and call out for me. I found my hope again as I climbed out of bed. I hoped my prayers would be heard and answered.

*****

I yawned hard, making my eyes water with the force of the sudden exhaustion. It had been a long day. Taking time off had been great for me but I'd quickly gotten out of diner mode. Coming back to work on a Friday had been stupid. I should have taken the whole week off because today had flat worn me out.

I yawned again and went back to cleaning the counter. It was almost closing time. There wasn't a single customer lingering at a table over the remnants of their meal. As I cleaned I kept one eye on the big windows, watching out front for the lights on the second floor of the bakery to come on. Then I'd know Joy and Will were home. Then I'd know the trial was over for the day. Maybe then she'd text me and let me know how it went.

When the bells on the door chimed, I looked up, ready to tell the visitor the kitchen was already closed for the day. I didn't have to say anything though. I just smiled.

"Hey, sis," Tres said as he slipped behind the counter. He quickly gave me a big hug then crossed behind me, slipping into the kitchen to see Dad. When he returned, he was eating an ice cream sandwich.

"Those are for your niece, not you."

"She told me it was okay."

I laughed at him. Ria loved her uncle Tres but I knew full well she wouldn't have shared anything with him. She was right in the middle of a super selfish phase I was eager for her to outgrow. Tres boosted himself up onto my clean counter and grinned at me. I rolled my eyes and gave up on cleaning. Tres wasn't going to be any help.

"So what's up, big brother?" I hopped onto the counter next to him, sticking one finger into his ice cream and scooping out a taste for myself.

"I spent the past two days over in Windsor at the courthouse."

"I know." My heart clenched and froze. For a second I was ice cold. I'd managed to forget about it for a while again. I didn't want to think about it now.

"Yeah. I feel like I should. For him." His voice broke and I reached over, caught one of his hands and laced my fingers with his. My strong, tough big brother. He missed Mateo as much as I did.

"I'm glad you did. I couldn't do it."

"I know. He'd understand why. I do too. If I was in your shoes. If it had been Mallie." Tres stopped, ate a bite of the ice cream sandwich, composed himself. "The second day was rough. Harder than yesterday. They started talking about—"

"Don't. You don't have to say anything." I looked away from him, focusing on the collection of ketchup and mustard bottles across from us. The red and yellow bottles blurred when my eyes started to fill with tears. I blinked again and again, fast and hard, pushing away those unwelcome tears.

"Anyway," Tres said. He sighed and gave me a quick, one-armed hug before he slipped back to the floor. "Anyway, it was interesting. Not like the trials you see on the TV shows."

"Oh, yeah."

"Yesterday was mostly reading the charges and listing the witnesses to be called and going over evidence. After the lunch break, the prosecutor tried to start with a breakdown of the whole crime spree from last year. The defense lawyer got all mad and they yelled at each other. Not much happened afterward. The judge dismissed everyone for the day and took the lawyers to his chambers. I guess they were fighting about what can and cannot be included in the trial. They were really nasty to each other today. Lots of interrupting each other. The judge yelled at them several times."

"Sounds like one sort of boring day followed by one sort of not good day."

"That sums it up. One thing has been strange though."

"What?" I asked as I slid to the floor and picked back up my cleaning rag. I wiped down the counter where we'd been sitting then tossed it into the laundry bucket under the counter.

"Teo's folks haven't been there either day. Or his sister."

"What? Really? That is strange. The last text I got from Tia said she planned to fly out and be there."

"That's what I thought you'd told me. As I was driving home, I got to thinking. I haven't seen their folks in several months. Have you?"

I thought for a moment, trying to remember the last time I'd seen my in-laws. Even though I'd racked my brain a few days earlier at the cemetery I tried again. I still couldn't remember seeing them in the diner or at the grocery store or anywhere in town since . . . July maybe.

"No, no I haven't."

"Have you texted or called either of them?"

I looked away at his question. I'd thought for a bit that I'd done better with them but Tres' question made me realize I hadn't. Our less-than-good relationship was just as much my fault as it was theirs. When he'd been alive, Teo had made us talk to each other. It had been easy to let things fall apart when they'd taken their first trip out of town. I'd assumed they'd reach out sooner or later. At least to see Ria.

"I haven't. I'm a horrible person. I just got tired of having to work so hard with them." He gave me a look but didn't say anything. Tres had been on the Baca's bad list since he was thirteen. He and Teo had gotten suspended after a prank Tres had cooked up backfired. Those two knew how to hold a grudge.

"One of us should go check on them," he finally said.

"I'll go tomorrow. Take Ria. They're nice to me when I bring her."

"Good. Okay. I've gotta go. Mallie tried to go back to work today. I want to get home. I'm betting she overdid it and is exhausted."

I smiled at him. I had wanted my brother and my best friend to realize they loved each other for ages. Now that they were married it filled me up with happy. Two of my favorite people, making a beautiful life together.

"Hug her for me and try to make her stay home tomorrow. She's not even two weeks out from surgery. She shouldn't be working yet."

"I know that and you know that but getting her to agree to it is a completely different thing."

I laughed and agreed then followed him to the door, locking it behind him. I flipped off the OPEN sign, then started working my way around all the windows, lowering the blinds. I promised myself I'd go see Teo's parents tomorrow. I could take them lunch. They always loved our loaded cheeseburgers and our chili-cheese fries. It would be good to see them. I hadn't been doing a very good job of including them in their granddaughter's life. Tomorrow would be my first step toward fixing that.

Chapter Seventeen

I took a long lunch break the next day to go check on my in-laws. All night I'd thought on what Tres had brought to my attention. It had been in the back of my head that I hadn't seen them in months. He made me face it. Where had they been? How had I let them slip out of my mind? I felt like a horrible person for letting so much time pass. I should have been bringing Ria over to see them once a week. Making them dinner. Something to spend time with them. We were living with the same loss. I should have been helping them through it.

I got a huge surprise when I pulled into their driveway. A for sale sign stood in their front yard. I quickly climbed out of the car and gathered up Maria and the bag of burgers I'd brought them. I rang the doorbell once, twice, three times and got no answer. Worry and panic started to flood me so I returned Ria to her car seat, buckled her in, and put the food back in the car.

Returning to the house, I rang the doorbell several more times. Nothing. I stepped back into the yard and stared at the house, processing. It looked so similar to the house I'd grown up in. A long, low brick ranch. Big front windows with perfectly trimmed boxwood hedges below them. I'd spent a lot of happy hours inside. Celebrated birthdays and holidays and anniversaries. It felt five kinds of wrong to me now. Like the light had gone out of it. Like the life had gone out of it. I climbed into one of the hedges, pressing my face to the glass.

Empty.

The whole house was empty.

I couldn't understand what I was seeing. Where were they? What had happened? I pulled out my cell as I climbed out of the bushes, quickly pulling up Teo's sister and pressing the call button.

"Tia, hey it's Luz. I'm standing in front of your parents' house and it's empty with a for sale sign in the yard. What's going on?"

Silence. Then a sigh.

"I thought they'd told you, Luz. I'm sorry. They're moving. Out here. They say Rio Verde is haunted. The house is haunted. They see Mateo everywhere. They—" She stopped herself, ending her final sentence too soon.

"They what, Tia? They what?"

Another sigh.

"They blame you. They said Teo told them he'd taken the job at the truck stop because it paid better than any of the places in town. He told them you needed a new car and the truck stop job would get you one faster. They think he would never have walked in on the robbery if he hadn't been working there."

It was my turn to go silent. She'd blindsided me. I'd suspected as much but to hear it said out loud, to have it confirmed. The sunny front yard with the scattering of fall leaves spun around me, blurring. I stepped backward to the porch and sat down hard, the impact from the concrete vibrating up my back, making me wince.

"I know it wasn't your fault. They do too, deep down inside. They're grieving and angry. The trial is coming up. It set them off. They didn't want to be there for it. I think they'll think more clearly out here. The distance will do them some good."

"It started already."

"What?"

"The trial. It started two days ago. Tres is going every day. He felt like someone should be there to represent Mateo. He was shocked when he didn't see your parents there. I thought they would be there. I thought you would be there, too."

She was quiet again. I could feel her guilt coming through the phone. She knew she and her parents should have been there. So should I. Suddenly it felt like we'd all failed him.

"What about Maria?" She was my first clear, rational thought. "She has lost her father. Now her grandparents. It's cruel of them to do this to her."

"I know and I agree, Luz. I've said that to them. I've said that and more. I can't change how they're feeling right now. I'm on your side but they're my parents. I have to take care of them right now."

From her side of the call, I heard a bang and a small voice call out "Mom!"

"Oh, crap. The dog just knocked the fishbowl off the table. I've got to go, Luz. I'll keep in touch and I'll keep working on them. Let me know how the trial goes, okay? Thank Tres for representing the family."

I stared at my phone, watching until the screen went dark, then tossed it into the grass in front of me. I couldn't move. I couldn't think.

"How could they think this was all my fault?" I asked my question to the empty front yard. My first instinct was to call Mallie but couldn't make myself pick up my discarded phone. I thought about calling my mom or Isabel but couldn't bring myself to call them, either. I stared at my phone for a while, then pushed myself up from the porch, grabbed it, and headed to my car. Ria was starting to fuss and I had to get back to the diner. I had to go pretend everything was fine.

Chapter Eighteen

I went straight to Mallie and Tres' house when I got off work. All afternoon, the truth Tia had revealed had stuck in my head. I turned it over and over all day until I couldn't let it go so I went to Mallie. Talking to Mallie always set things right in my head. Plus, it would keep my mind off the Tate House and all the looming, unanswered questions it carried. What would happen if we got it? What would happen if we didn't? What if we got it and it turned into a huge money pit? Or the bed and breakfast idea totally failed? The reality of attempting something so huge had totally overshadowed my excitement. So I was headed to Mallie's.

Maybe she could help settle my racing mind and keep my focus off the trial and everything it stirred up. Even a few minutes with my best friend would be a blessing today. I pulled up to their house as the sun was setting. For a bit, I sat in my car. The hayfield across from the house was dotted with the last bales of the year. Tres must have spent all of Saturday baling. The pale, yellow-green blocks caught the sunlight and flamed golden. The cottonwood trees flanking the field and the river beyond the house still carried a sprinkling of bright yellow leaves, most blown off by fall winds. The two crowning jewels sat between the fields and the trees. A huge barn in deep red brick with a shining steel roof—through the open door I could see the tractor and a stack of hay. Across from the barn was a beautiful old Victorian house. I remembered how it had once looked. Worn down. Forgotten. Mallie and her dad had transformed it, breathing life back into the building, turning it into a home again.

The front door opened and Mallie appeared, balanced on crutches, right knee wrapped in a brace that started well above her knee and reached all the way down to her foot.

"Come on in, Lucy Lou," she called, crossing the front porch and stopping at the stairs.

"Don't you dare come down those stairs," I said as I stepped out.

"I'm not going to. Your brother would yell at me."

I laughed and released Ria from her car seat. She hit the ground running and headed right for Mallie.

"Careful! Don't hurt your Auntie," I called, sighing when she slowed and carefully walked up and hugged Mallie.

"Uncle T. is in the kitchen. Go get him. He's got cookies." Ria shot into the house. We heard Tres greet her and then a peal of giggles. He'd keep her entertained for hours. Tres was still a big kid himself sometimes.

Mallie swung herself down the porch to a long, low bench sitting under the living room window. I followed her and helped her sit, then sat beside her. We didn't talk. I just leaned against her, soaking in the best friend mojo we'd always generated when we were together.

"What's up, Luz?"

I sighed, not sure how to explain it all. Finally, I spilled it all out, laying my afternoon at her feet. She didn't say a word when I finished, staring out toward the now-dark hayfield instead.

"That's messed up," she said.

"I know, right?"

"What are you going to do?"

"What can I do?"

"Probably nothing."

"I thought you'd say something along those lines."

"You just needed me to agree with you?"

"Yes. I kept thinking I should call them. Or write a letter. Or even fly to Phoenix and talk to them face to face."

"The Bacas are two of the most stubborn, hard-headed people I've ever met. I will never understand how Mateo and Tia grew up to be so easy going and chill. There is nothing you can do—that anyone can do—to change their minds until they *want* to change their minds. You've got to wait them out."

"I'm horrible at waiting."

"I know Miss I-Couldn't-Wait-An-Extra-Six-Months-To-Get-Married."

I laughed at her. She had a point. My impatience was a big reason Teo and I had eloped.

"So wait them out?"

"Yup."

"Are there really cookies in the kitchen?"

"Yup. Not any cookies either. Aunt Jo's cookies. Come on, before your kid and my husband eat them all." I had to smile as I followed Mallie into the house. Mallie's Aunt Jo making her cookies— that wouldn't have happened a few years ago. As awful as it had been when Mallie's mom died, an amazing amount of good had come into the world because of her departure. I had to hope at least some good would come about because Teo had been taken from me.

*****

I drove home with a lighter heart that evening. Mallie was right—I needed to wait it out. Wait out Teo's parents. Wait out the murder trial. Wait out an answer on the Tate House.

Good things come to those who wait.

I heard the words as clearly as if someone had spoken them. Teo had always said them to me when I got impatient. Like Mallie, he was right. I needed to wait. I'd waited for years to fall in love and I'd gotten him and then Maria. I looked back over my shoulder at her. Sound asleep. My precious girl. She was growing up to be more and more like her daddy with each day. Before long, she'd be grown up enough to tell me to wait and be patient too.

As I followed the familiar route home the last thing Mallie had told me came back to me. We'd stood shoulder to shoulder on the porch before I left, watching the stars wink on. *Pray about it, Luz. Pray about all of it*. She'd given me a hug next, kissed a sleeping Ria, and hobbled her way inside without saying anything else. I hadn't been good about praying since I'd begged God for Teo's life in the hospital. The only time I'd prayed in earnest was the other day when I'd prayed about the trial. I started to list out all the things I was carrying around in my heart. My aching grief. The desire to be rid of it. Worries about raising Maria alone. Worries about not getting the Tate House. And then worries about actually getting the Tate House. A growing desire to quit working at the RWB. Fear about breaking my parents' hearts if I did quit working at the diner. The list got very long very fast. I surprised myself. Until I'd started laying it all out I hadn't realized everything I was holding onto.

Once I got home I quickly tucked Ria into bed and grabbed a pad and paper. I needed to make the list real. Concrete. Visible.

By the time I started to fall asleep at the kitchen table I had used up all the pages in the little scratch pad and had even put a few things on the cardboard backing. I felt emptied out. Hollow. I turned out the lights and carried the sheets of paper to the bedroom with me. Once I'd checked on Ria and gotten myself ready for bed, I was ready to take on my lists a second time.

I turned on the little lamp on my nightstand and knelt on the floor with my lists. I stayed there until my knees ached and the cold floor had made me shiver. I stayed there until I'd gotten all the way through the list, praying about every single thing on it.

I didn't feel empty anymore. I felt something else.

Settled.

Settled and somehow freed.

Chapter Nineteen

Sunday dawned icy cold. I'd gone without a coat the whole day yesterday. Today, not so much. It was a coat-on kind of day. The start of winter might have been more than a month away but the Texas weather was already flirting with the idea of turning cold. I checked the forecast for the coming week as I gathered up clothes for Ria and me to wear. As I'd guessed, tomorrow it was supposed to warm right back up to Indian summer type temperatures. I loved Texas, couldn't imagine living anywhere else, but the crazy weather did kind of wear on me. Especially when I had to battle with a toddler about putting on a warm coat after having battled her on the long-sleeved dress and the warm tights. If Mallie hadn't made me promise to come to church, I would have given up and let her go back to watching cartoons in her pajamas.

By the time I dropped Ria off at the nursery, I was hoping for a nice long service so I could get a good break from little miss terrible-twos. She didn't look back at me, instead heading right in to play. The wild child who'd fought with me was gone. She loved being with the other kids at church. She was a social butterfly, just like her dad had been. Teo had never met a stranger and it looked like his daughter was going to grow up to be the same way.

I lingered back by the kids for a bit, then ducked into the kitchen to grab a bottle of water. As I finally made my way into the group of folks milling around outside the sanctuary door, I was surprised to not get any of the "so sorry for your loss" comments I'd grown used to. Instead everyone was whispering about the Tate House. It wasn't often that one of the grand old houses of Rio Verde went on the market. It made me a little sad to hear everyone talking about it. With this many folks discussing the house, there was going to be a lot of people interested in buying it. I wondered if Carson and I even had a chance of getting it.

I was feeling sort of melancholy by the time I made my way to the row up near the front where I always sat. Will and Joy were already there, both welcoming me with hugs. Carson sat down right after me, a vaguely sad expression on his face that probably mirrored my own. He'd probably heard the talk about the Tate House too. Tres appeared right after him, without Mallie in tow. I wondered where she was as the music started and I stood to sing with everyone.

The music ended quicker than normal and everyone sat. I looked around as subtly as I could, still not sure where Mallie was or why she'd wanted me here if she wasn't. I tried to ask my brother but he shushed me and smiled, then nodded to the stage.

Dr. Bell took the stage with a big smile. He adjusted the small microphone pinned to the lapel of his suit and welcomed everyone to Rio Verde First Baptist Church.

"We're starting a new sermon series today. I know you all noticed the musical portion was a little bit shorter. Don't worry, that doesn't mean I'm going to be talking longer. I'm actually going to be sharing duties with different folks over the next few weeks." He paused, picking up his worn leather Bible from the pulpit, turning to a marked section. "In Hebrews ten, verse twenty-two, it says, 'Let us continue to come near with sincere hearts in the full assurance that faith provides, because our hearts have been sprinkled clean from a guilty conscience, and our bodies have been washed with pure water.' God wants us to walk with Him. In all we do, we should be walking the path the Lord has laid out for us. So that's what we're going to talk about for the next few weeks. We'll start each week with a testimony. Members of the congregation will share stories of their walk with the Lord. Today, we're starting with a member of my own family because she was the easiest one to boss into doing this. Mallie, will you please come share your story?"

I was caught off guard when Mallie came out from backstage. Even on crutches she looked beautiful. Happy. Relaxed. But she'd always loved being on a stage. That's why ballet had suited her so well. She never had a bit of trouble with people watching her. I was surprised to see she had a Bible tucked under her arm. I recognized it—it had been her mother's. On the collar of her sweater was a little lapel mic like Dr. Bell's. He sat two stools in the center of the stage, let Mallie get comfortable on it, and then took her crutches away.

I looked over at Tres for an explanation but he just smiled and covered my hand with his.

"So, I'm sure all of y'all know me, but in case someone doesn't, I'm Mallie Martinez. I'm Dr. Bell's niece. I grew up in this church, always sitting right there on the second row where my husband and friends are sitting now." She smiled and gave us a little wave.

"I also grew up dancing. My parents put me in ballet classes as soon as I could walk. I was a goner right away. After graduating from Rio Verde High—go Bulldogs—I headed to New York City and the Juilliard School. By the time I graduated, I was headed toward what would have probably been an amazing dance career. That was all taken away when I was crushed between two cars while crossing a busy street. In an instant, I lost everything I'd been working toward. As I healed, I turned away from everything that had once been important. Dance. My friends. My family. The Lord."

Mallie paused and took a quick drink from a bottle of water Dr. Bell had set on a second stool within her reach.

"Four years ago, everything changed in my world again. Thanks to another car accident. Four years ago my mom died." Her voice broke and my heart cringed. I felt tears fill my eyes and fought the urge to go up there and hug her. "My mom died and we hadn't spoken in nearly six months. I never got to say sorry for how I'd acted. I never got to tell her how much she meant to me. So I came home. I came home and worked hard to right all the wrongs I'd done while I was so angry."

"My best friend, Luz Baca, has always told me about 'God things.' She has always been able to step back and see God's hand in things, guiding lives. Losing my mom wasn't a God thing but coming home was. I didn't even realize I had started to walk with God until I'd been back for several months. God led me to a career I love. God led me to a house that I helped save and I now call home. God led me to a family I thought I'd lost and the love of my life. God led me back to my faith."

She paused again and lifted the Bible. "This was my mom's Bible. I don't know if y'all do this, but Mom was a note taker. She always made notes in her Bible. Thoughts, quotes from sermons, all that sort of stuff. One of her notes says—and I'm paraphrasing because I can't for the life of me find it again— every memory of God's goodness keeps us walking with Him and keeps us remembering the people who help keep us on the right path. All the years after my accident when I was alone with my anger, God was walking with me. Even though I was mad at Him and the rest of the world, He was there. I just couldn't see Him. I couldn't see all the goodness in my life He had given me. But it was there. I had to lose my mom to learn that, but I know she'd be glad I finally got the message."

Mallie smiled and slipped off the stool. Dr. Bell stepped forward to hug her, hand her back her crutches, and take back over the service. As he started to speak, Mallie slipped into our row, climbing over Tres and sitting down beside me.

I hugged her tight and whispered in her ear, "I love you, I'm proud of you, and I needed to hear that. Thank you."

"I thought you did," she whispered back. "And I love you, too, Lucy Lou."

Chapter Twenty

I cornered Mallie as soon as church was over, catching the sleeve of her sweater and tugging her down the hallway toward the nursery. "Why didn't you tell me you were going to do that?"

She followed me with ease, a pro on her crutches. Getting a moment with her quickly proved to be nearly impossible though. People kept stopping us to hug her and tell her what her testimony had meant to them. After being stopped for the fourth time, I finally whispered I'd see her for lunch at my house and left her with the trio of gray-haired ladies who kept hugging her.

With Ria in tow, I raced home to pick up her toys and pull all my extra chairs into the den. It was my turn to have our weekly after-church lunch, something I had totally forgotten about until the church service ended. I knew no one would care if the house was neat and tidy, but I still flew around each room, picking up and cleaning quickly.

I looked around my little house—our little house—committing each detail to memory. If—great big if—the Tate House did become mine I'd be leaving this house. It was the only home Teo and I had shared together. I would be sad to leave it, but a big part of me was growing excited by the possibility of moving on to something new. It would be a bittersweet goodbye when the time came. I'd never have another first house with Teo. I'd never have another first house with Ria. This would always be a special little house. Hopefully, it would be the stage for more firsts for another family. Hopefully, Maria and I would have lots of firsts in the Tate House.

I didn't have time to dwell on any of my conflicting emotions though. I'd just sat Ria on the den rug with a cup juice when the front door opened and Tres and Mallie barged in carrying a stack of pizza boxes.

"Joy and Will are right behind us with drinks," Tres said, pausing to give me a one-armed hug. "Our sisters are coming, too, supposedly with dessert."

"Oh, I hope Marisol made brownies. No one can beat her brownies. They're amazing. Don't either of you tell Joy I said that; she's awful proud of her brownies too." I took the pizzas from Tres and set them out on the table, adding a stack of paper plates and a roll of paper towels.

"Mallie Jo, you come let me hug you," I demanded. Mallie didn't hesitate. I hugged her long and hard and when we let go we were both teary-eyed. "I am so stinking proud of you, Mal. Everything you said was so beautiful and you were so brave to open up like that to the whole church."

Tres stepped up behind her and hugged her. "That's my girl. So brave."

For a second I stepped back and watched them. I loved how they loved each other. I'd always wanted my brother to find someone who was a perfect match for him. I'd always wanted the same thing for my best friend. I just couldn't stop marveling on the fact that they'd found that in each other.

"Hey, y'all." It was Will pushing through the front door with two grocery bags of two-liter drinks.

"Hey back. Come on in." I rushed over to take the drinks from him while Mallie and her crutches moved out of the way. Behind me, I heard Tres scoop up Ria and I smiled. He loved his niece. I couldn't wait for Mallie and him to get started on their plan to adopt. My brother was built to be a dad.

"Oh my gosh, Joy, what are you wearing?" Mallie's shocked question pulled me away from the cooler I'd set beside the table.

Joy stopped in the doorway, bag of ice in each hand, and grinned at us. She didn't look very different than normal. She was in a pair of worn jeans and running shoes. The shirt she was wearing though was new. It read, "I am so pregnant." She smiled at us as we took in what she was announcing.

"No way," Mallie finally said.

"Yes way," she said, looking across the room at Will. His smile said it all. It was a grinning-ear-to-ear-dad-to-be smile. I'd never seen him happier. Or Joy, either. Even Carson, who'd walked in behind Joy and was smiling like a kid at Christmas. Joy was like a sister to him. I guessed that meant he was going to be an uncle.

Mallie let out a whoop of joy and gave Joy a hug, turning to Will, lingering on his hug longer. They were more siblings than cousins. She knew better than anyone how much Will had longed to be a dad.

Before we sat down to eat, Joy's half-sister Lane walked in. "You're wearing it," she said when she spotted Joy's shirt. She'd known before us. It made me happy they'd gotten so close. They'd never known the other existed until Joy moved to Rio Verde, but no one would ever guess that they hadn't grown up together.

Will and Tres dove into the pizza, Joy quickly following. Before I could fill a plate, Isabel and Marisol walked in, derailing my plans to fill my own stomach. Tres reacted like a typical big brother and threw one of Ria's toys at Marisol. She had been dodging things Tres had thrown all her life and had amazing reflexes; she caught the stuffed fish and hurled it right back at him.

"Your brother," Isabel said, setting down the pan of brownies she carried.

"Your sister," I said, giving her a hug. "I missed you at church this morning, Is."

"I missed being at church. I couldn't convince this new furniture guy to deliver my stuff any other time than this morning. It was worth it though. Mallie, you'll love the stuff I got. Several pieces will totally work for that little Craftsman you're just finishing up for the Thomas family."

Mallie and Isabel filled their plates and joined everyone else in the den. I made a plate for me and another for Mari and joined them.

She was distracted by Maria, having stolen her from Tres after she'd finished chucking toys at him. I sat on the floor, leaning my back against Tres' legs and stayed quiet, letting the talk flow around me. Tres answered questions about his farm, Will filled everyone in on the ever-present drama going on at the Rio Verde Bank. Mallie and Isabel talked about the latest house restoration project they were working on. Joy filled us in on everything with her bakery while Marisol made us all laugh with stories about the events over at the RWB. Carson shared stories of his hiking adventures. Ria got passed around, stole bits of pizza, and got loved on.

"I love y'all," I blurted out, stopping all the conversation in an instant. "I mean it. I love y'all. I don't know how I would have made it through the past year without you."

Joy raised her cup and added, "I second that. I love all of you. I would never have stayed here and found my family if it wasn't for each of you."

Mallie smiled and expanded on the theme. "I third it. I could never have gotten to where I am without any of you."

"Oh my gosh, y'all are all so sappy today. Mal, you're not allowed to give speeches at church, no matter how much my dad badgers you." Will broke the spell, cracking us all up.

The afternoon faded into evening quickly. We ate more pizza than any of us should have and everyone eventually headed back to their own homes. Ria conked out as the last car drove away, giving me a quiet house.

"They all miss you, babe." I spoke with my face raised up, sending my words toward Heaven. I'd felt Mateo nearby the whole time everyone had been here. "I hope you're on board with this big change I'm trying to make. I'm scared to take on something like this without you by my side. I'm going to need you to reach out to God and get Him to help me out."

Chapter Twenty-One

Monday afternoon, by the end of my shift at the diner, I had myself convinced we'd lost the Tate House. There had been no phone call from the realtor. No news at all. I wanted to pull up the listing for the house online, but I was too chicken. I was sure it would say **OFF THE MARKET**. I went home and started laundry, ready to have a pity party for the rest of the day. Carson had other ideas though.

I had an armful of wet towels and a sobbing toddler clinging to my leg when the doorbell rang.

"Its open," I shouted, secretly hoping whoever it was would hear Ria crying and run the other way. Instead, Carson appeared in the laundry room doorway, his arrival announced by noisy footsteps and the jingle of his car keys. Joy had been right; the man couldn't walk quietly.

"Need help?"

"Bless you," I said as I shoved the towels at him. He caught them, stepping aside when I picked up Ria. She'd hit melt-down mode and was now screaming as she sobbed.

"What set her off?"

"Her blanket is in with the towels. I thought I had time to wash and dry it while she napped but I was clearly wrong." I held her close, rubbing her back, trying to soothe her. As I walked away I heard the dryer start and thanked God for Carson and his great timing. She finally started to calm, her sobbing shifting into hiccups.

"I'm sorry, *mija*, but your blanket was so dirty."

"No, Mama." She hiccupped. "Want."

"Nope. Ask right."

She leaned back and frowned at me but tried again. "Want my blanket."

93

"Soon, Ria. How about a snack first?" Her face finally switched back to her normal happy smile. My girl loved her food. I set her down in a chair and gave her a cup of applesauce. I handed her a spoon and smiled when she used it. She had been fighting spoons and forks, preferring fingers.

"So, bad time?"

Carson. He was watching us from a safe distance.

"No. We're good now, right, Maria?" She ignored me and kept shoving food in her mouth. "What's up?"

"Well," he started, joining me at the table and tossing a real estate listings book in front of me. "I figure we've missed out on the Tate House since we haven't heard from Sandie yet. I don't think we should give up though. We've got a good idea and I think we'd be a good team. So let's look at some other houses. There has to be more than one potential bed and breakfast around here. Maybe we could find a place in the country, make it a retreat type of space. We've got options."

"I'd really planned to eat junk food tonight and feel sorry for myself. Probably pull up the listing for the Tate House on my laptop, feel sad."

"Boring. Let's do this instead."

"Fine, but I have to do laundry, too." A spoon went skidding across the table, interrupting us. Carson reacted fast and caught it before it hit the floor.

"I'll help. Entertain the kid."

"Okay. Let's look. I'll get my laptop. It'll be easier than sharing that little book." I cleaned up Ria and turned her lose. She toddled into the den, right to her toys. I was lucky with her. She played by herself so well. I'd seen other kids her age pester their parents or siblings constantly. She was so independent. When she started to walk she'd pushed me away, wanting to do it on her own. Her independence was nice now but I knew it would make her a handful later.

We spent the rest of the day on the couch, sharing the laptop, looking at real estate. Ria would come sit with us, climbing from one lap to the other, sitting for a while, then going back to play. We took a lot of breaks. For laundry. For snacks. To play with Ria. By the time Carson went home, we hadn't found an alternative for the Tate House. We'd had a good day though.

Once Ria was tucked in and I was tucked in too, I thought back over the afternoon. It had been beautifully normal. Two friends, hanging out, working on a project. No mention of the sad baggage we both carried around. No sad glances. The trial never came up with Carson even though Tres had texted me an update while he'd been here. None of the conversation topics I had to work to avoid with other people ever slipped into my afternoon with Carson. It had been full of houses and dreams of future business success. It was the most normal an afternoon I'd had since Teo had been killed. It had been exactly what I'd needed. A blessing of a day. I'd felt like a normal person.

I rolled over and reached for my phone. I pulled up my pictures, finding one of Mateo. He was frozen in mid-laugh. I couldn't remember what I'd done to get him to laugh. It was my favorite picture of him. One of my favorites, really. I had another one, in a frame in Ria's room, of him holding her for the first time. I held on to those pictures, preferring to remember him in those frozen moments rather than the way I'd last seen him alive. He'd been pale and in so much pain, about to be rushed into surgery. He'd made them stop so he could talk to me. He'd told me he loved me. Told me where to find important papers. Told me to be strong and tell Ria he loved her too. I hadn't wanted to admit it at the time but looking back I could tell, he'd known he wouldn't make it. He'd still made sure to take care of us in those last few seconds together.

Something told me he was still taking care of me. He and the Big Guy. Before all this had happened, I would have been able to see God's hand in everything. In the red light that made me miss an accident. In the kindness of a random stranger that brightened a bad day. I'd seen God working all around me.

Now I wondered if I'd been imagining the abandoned feeling I'd carried with me since Teo died. I thought for a moment and wondered if God's hand had been in Carson deciding to stay. In the Tate House going up for sale. I wondered if Teo was up there in Heaven, working with the Big Guy to keep me moving forward.

"Are you doing this?" I asked the picture. "Is this you?"

I got no answer but I hadn't expected one. I tossed the phone on the nightstand and settled back into bed. As I started to drift off, Carson came to mind. I thought about how much Teo would have liked him. I liked him, too. After hanging out with him, I felt like I'd known him forever. I'd been happy to see him today. As I thought about it, my heart skipped a beat. Just one quickly missed beat. I wondered what all that was about as I drifted off to sleep.

Chapter Twenty-Two

"Where is your cell phone?" Carson shouted, storming into the RWB. The lunch rush was starting and I cringed when the place went quiet and people stared.

"I'll get your order right out to you," I said to the table of teens from the high school I'd been helping.

Carson followed me as I slipped behind the counter and passed the order to my dad. He glared at Carson who, wisely, retreated to the proper side of the counter.

"What would you like for lunch, Carson?"

"I'd like to know why you haven't answered your phone. I've been calling you for an hour."

I gestured to the diner full of people. He looked around and he finally registered all the people eating.

"We've been kinda busy, dude," Marisol said as she passed Dad another order, then headed to the register to ring someone up.

"Did I just make a scene?"

"A small one, yes." A new customer claimed the stool beside him so I stepped over, took his drink order and handed him a menu. "Why are you so wound up?" I handed the man his drink and returned to my spot in front of Carson.

"She called."

"Who?"

"Sandie."

"Sandie the realtor? That Sandie?"

Carson smiled at me and nodded. "The very one."

"What did she want?" I leaned closer, dropping my voice to a whisper. I still hadn't told my folks about the plan. Didn't want Dad to find out this way.

"She wants to meet with us. She and Miss Patsy."

"No."

"Yes."

"Do you think we got it?"

"Sure looks like it."

I wanted to scream and jump up and down. Or run around the diner and hug everyone. Or dance around and throw confetti in the air.

"Order up, Luz."

I couldn't celebrate. I had to go back to work. I grabbed my order and headed to the waiting customers. I bumped Carson's arm with mine as I passed him, the plates on my tray clinking together quietly.

"I can be free by two o'clock."

He nodded and pulled out his cell phone. I heard him say hello to Sandie as I walked away.

*****

"So why did I need to meet you at Miss Patsy's house?"

"It isn't Miss Patsy's house anymore." I boosted myself onto the hood of my car. I didn't look at Mallie. Instead looked at the historical marker to the right of my car. I knew the history of the house, but I skimmed the brass plate anyway. Built in 1890. The first brick house to be built in Rio Verde. Home to the Tate family for generations. Until today, the last fact hadn't changed.

"What do you mean it isn't Miss Patsy's house anymore?" Mallie carefully sat on the bumper to the left of me, leaning her crutches against the car. She guarded her healing knee, keeping the brace-clad joint straight, her foot resting on the sidewalk. She gave me a bump with her shoulder, an easy, deeply familiar gesture. One I loved. I bumped her back before I spoke again.

"It just sold."

"When? Did you get it?"

I looked at her but didn't say anything.

"So who bought the house? The rumor mill said over twenty offers were put in. Please say y'all got it."

"We did. Fifty-fifty partners." The whole neighborhood went silent when I let the words drop. Ria got quiet. The birds stopped singing and for a split second, I thought Mallie had a heart attack.

I braved a glance over at her and was rewarded with an image I would hold in my head for the rest of my life. My best friend. Always quick with a comeback or a comment. Speechless. Her pale blue eyes were huge. Her mouth open in a perfect little round O. I fought the urge to pull out my cell phone and snap a picture. No one who knew Mallie Jo Andrews Martinez would believe me. No one had ever seen her without something to say.

"Mal, it's your turn to say something now."

"I . . . umm . . ." She looked away from me and stared up at the house. Finally, she tugged off her baseball cap and ran a hand through her messy hair. "Did you just say you now own the Tate House?"

"I did. You need a haircut. Come by the house tonight and I'll give you a trim."

"Okay, thanks. Wait, don't change the subject. You own the Tate House?"

"Fifty percent of it, yes."

"How can you and Carson afford it?"

"You won't believe it. Miss Patsy had this wild plan for how to sell it."

"She is a crazy old lady." Mallie shook her head and looked at the house again. I guessed she was picturing Miss Patsy. The last time I'd seen her, yesterday when she sold us the house, she'd had on what was, for her, a fancy outfit. A glittery black sweater, skinny jeans I was sure Marisol had donated to Goodwill a week ago, and her ever-present tall red boots. Miss Patsy was a character for sure.

"True, but she's not like, *crazy* crazy. She's unique but still totally in control of every itty bitty bit of her brain."

Mallie nodded and looked away from the house. The shock had finally faded from her face. Now she was totally keyed in on what I was saying. She was curious and excited. Mallie always loved a good story.

"Everyone who wanted to buy the house had to tell her a story. Not like a fairy tale but a story of what they thought their future in the house would be like—what sort of life they'd live in the house. The story she liked best would get to buy the house. For one hundred dollars."

"Shut. Up. Really?"

"Really."

Mallie studied me through narrowed eyes as she processed everything I'd said. I knew the exact moment she realized I hadn't told her why I'd asked her to meet me here. I could have told her this news anywhere. Her face shifted and a slow smiled spread across her face. A what-are-you-up-to kind of smile.

"Do you need a good contractor?"

I looked away and smiled up at the house. "As it so happens, we do."

Chapter Twenty-Three

Once the shock of my announcement had worn off, Mallie went into contractor mode. She pulled out her legal pad and a pencil and put on her tool belt. I packed up Ria and we hit the house, thankful Miss Patsy had given Carson and me access to the house for the day so we could get our plans moving. I followed Mallie from room to room as she tapped walls and thumped on floors with her crutches and did other contractor things. It was fun seeing her in her element. It still threw me a bit seeing my ballet dancer best friend wearing a tool belt and a baseball cap all day.

As we wandered the big house, one thing became very clear. It was in great shape. Mallie didn't find anything structurally wrong. All the things wrong were cosmetic. Mostly the wallpaper. All of the wallpaper. Gold floral wallpaper in the dining room. Deep maroon damask wallpaper surrounding the curved windows in the library. Floral patterned paper in the sitting room. Stripes in each bathroom. Fancy French toilet paper featuring a range of nature scenes in a sitting room. No room had the same wallpaper but almost every room had wallpaper.

"How do you feel about wallpaper?"

"I hate it so much," I answered with a laugh.

"Thank goodness, because it needs to go. You know, it's going to take a lot of work to get this stuff off of all the walls."

"I'm already on it." Carson's voice came echoing toward us from several rooms away.

Mallie started and looked around. "Where is he? I didn't even know he was in the house."

"Carson, where are you?" I yelled.

"Kitchen!" was the shouted reply.

We headed toward him, finding him in the rear staircase off the kitchen. Its walls were clad in a bright, lime green wallpaper. He'd been working while I'd met with Mallie. He'd been surprisingly successful too. A big section of the staircase was now bare, the dirty white plaster an improvement over the seventies-era paper.

"Wow," Mallie said, stepping around me to inspect the section of the wall Carson had freed from the hideous paper. She ran her hand over the plaster, then tapped a few places with her pencil. "Let's hope the rest of the plaster is in such good shape. If it is, there will be way less work to do before we can paint the walls."

"Excellent," said Carson as he carefully peeled up another section of paper. We watched as he worked until he could get a good hold on the paper. Once he could, he slowly pulled the paper up parallel to the wall, removing another big chunk with ease.

"How in the world did you learn how to remove wallpaper so well?" Mallie asked before I could. I was dying to know where this hidden talent had come from.

Carson laughed and sprayed another section of paper with some sort of magical formula. He sat on one of the steps and faced us. "I was a bad kid. Got into trouble a ton. Every time I got busted, my mom would loan me out to her friends to do chores. For like, all of high school, every single one of Mom's friends got into redecorating. Which meant stripping wallpaper. Lots of wallpaper. I got really good at removing it."

"So what's in the bottle?" I asked.

"My secret formula." He winked and my heart skipped a beat again. I took the bottle he was holding out, unscrewed the sprayer, and sniffed the contents.

"Dish soap?"

"Yup. Dish soap, hot water, and one of these things." He held up a little tool around the size of a fist with a ton of tiny pins on it. "This scores the paper and lets the soap and water get to the glue. You just score, soak, and scrape. Over and over and over."

Behind us, there was a sudden crash and a wailing cry.

"Ria," I said. Mallie jumped out of my way and I rushed into the kitchen where I'd left her playing with her ball. I found her under a pile of cookie sheets. "Baby, what happened?" A whimpering cry of "Mama" was my answer. I glanced at the clock on the huge, ancient microwave and saw it was way past time for her afternoon nap. I scooped her up and made my goodbyes, then headed to the front door. Mallie caught up to me in the front hallway.

"You're sure about all this?"

I glanced over and saw she'd shifted back into best friend mode. Her business-serious face was gone, replaced with her concerned-best-friend face. She was asking about a lot more than the house project. Was I sure about moving on to something so different? Was I sure about giving up the house Mateo and I had shared? Was I sure about leaving behind the family diner? She didn't have to ask those questions though. The simple question she had asked was enough. It covered all of those unasked questions and more.

"I'm sure, Mallie Jo. I have to move forward. I have to do something that's mine. I can't keep standing still. I can't stay in this sad place anymore. It's killing me." My voice broke and I looked away, resting my cheek on Ria's head. Mallie opened her arms and wrapped both of us in a hug. She didn't say anything else, only smiled and let me leave. I knew she'd keep my news to herself. She would know I needed to tell my family myself. That was one of the best things about having a friend who had known me my entire life. I could leave a lot of things unsaid.

I headed home and got Ria into bed for her nap. She was asleep before I'd turned out the light. Her whole world was about to change. Before Mallie had got there, Carson and I had worked out the living arrangements at the Tate House. Ria and I would take the little guest house in the back. Carson would take the old staff's quarters off the kitchen. The whole rest of the house would be for guests. Plenty of room. We had a big dining room for breakfast each day. Carson felt like he could shape up the garden and the yard in the spring. I sat down at the kitchen table, overwhelmed by the project in front of me. I reached for a handy scratchpad to start a to-do list but my hand landed on Teo's Bible instead. I didn't even remember setting it on the table yet there it was. I pulled it toward me and laid my head down on it. I remembered all the nights I'd fallen asleep while he sat up beside me, reading over things Dr. Bell had mentioned in a Sunday sermon. The Bible was everything to him. He loved all books, but his Bible was his compass, his bedtime story, his reference for all things. I sat up and opened it to a random page and started to read. I needed a compass of my own.

*****

I was so glad I'd taken the next morning off. Mom had given me a shopping list and the RWB business credit card. I was supposed to do the weekly shopping for the diner. My punishment for taking so much time off recently. I'd get right on it, too, right after a little detour.

"Daddy," Maria said when I turned into the Rio Verde Cemetery.

"You got it, Ria. We're going to visit your daddy."

I turned in at the main entrance, passing under the metal arch proclaiming the cemetery name. It sat on top of stone pillars, making the entrance fancy. I could remember when the entrance was only a break in the wooden fence marked by a hand-painted sign. The new entrance was at least eight years old and I still looked for the old, worn out sign every time I came here. I was as bad as my parents, I realized. Soon I'd be telling Ria back-in-my-day stories.

I drove as directly as possible to Teo's grave. The winding cemetery roads forced me to take a short scenic drive. I passed the hill where Mallie's mom, Tess, was buried. At the base of the same hill, in a fenced-in section by the road, was where Joy's grandparents were laid to rest. I guess that was part of getting older—knowing more and more of the cemetery's residents.

Teo's plot was easy to find. It was in a new section of the cemetery where the graves were marked, mostly, by plaques set flat in the ground. I'd had to battle the cemetery director to get a traditional, upright stone for his grave. It stuck out but made me happy. Leave it to my husband to find a way to stand out for eternity. I parked and set Ria down. She headed to the headstone, gave it a pat and said "Daddy," then went running off to play.

I sat in the grass before the marker, shifted so I could see Ria, then told Teo about my news. I ran through all of it, not missing a detail.

"I know you haven't heard me say this in a long time, but I think this may be a God thing. The way all the pieces fell together . . . it seems meant to be. As if God was guiding it all. I wish you could tell me if it was."

For a few minutes, I sat there, watching Ria chase leaves in the wind. I wished he was here. It hurt less, now, without him. I had to think the reason for the lessening of my grief was due to the Tate House. It sure seemed as though the sad, lonely old house was already healing my heart.

Chapter Twenty-Four

"Mom, Dad, do you have a bit of time? I need to talk to you about something." I was terrified to tell them. This was so much scarier than telling them Teo and I had eloped and were pregnant— and that had been the running-from-a-horror-movie-killer kind of scary. It was now or never though. The diner was quiet. Finally. For the first time all day. I'd been stalling the whole time. It had only been around twenty-four hours since Carson and I got the Tate House. We didn't even have signed paperwork yet. I felt horrible. I felt like I was lying to my parents. It was assumed by everyone in the family that Marisol and I would one day take over the diner. Instead, I was going to desert the family business. I was going to leave them short-handed.

Mallie had been texting once an hour to see if she could stop keeping the secret. I knew she was excited. Not only for me but for her. To be able to add renovating such a huge, historic home to her newly created company website would be a huge boost to her business. She had dreams of getting Andrews and Andrews Restoration into all of the big home improvement magazines. Maybe even on TV. She'd only told Tres and me, but we both knew if anyone could do something so big from little Rio Verde, Texas, it would be Mallie. Since she'd gotten her feet and faith back under her, she'd gone back to being the unstoppable force she'd been as a kid.

I wished I had the same sort of confidence in myself. I was taking on the challenge of turning the Tate House into a B and B, but I still didn't know if I was heading in the right direction. I thought it might be a God thing, but my conviction was at war with my doubts. It was a huge, scary thing to take on. I'd never tackled anything like it. The project was something to focus on though. I was hoping Carson and Miss Patsy were right. I hoped the project would help turn off the

106

broken and sad part of me, so I could maybe forget about grieving for a while. Maybe if I was super busy all the noise, all the bad dreams, and all the empty sadness would finally go away. Maybe my hurting heart would finally heal and maybe, like Mallie, I'd discover what I was supposed to be doing with my life.

But before I could do any of those things I had to quit the diner.

I stalled a little bit longer, watching them take advantage of the quiet and tidy up the kitchen. Our newly hired cook, my uncle Martin, had already headed home for the night, knowing the lull was really the end of business for the day. Mom and Dad could have taken a break too, enjoyed the lull. But they never stayed still when we were open. If Dad wasn't cooking he was cleaning. If Mom wasn't cleaning she was restocking the kitchen. They loved this place and put everything they had into it. As I looked on, Mom wiped down the grills with a cleaning rag and tossed the dirty rag to Dad, who threw it into a nearby rag bucket. For the first time, I noticed the sprinkling of gray at his temples and in his mustache. When had he started to look old? I glanced at Mom and caught her stretching and putting a hand on her back. When had she started to have back pain? I realized that since I'd married and moved out, I had stopped paying close attention to my parents.

I'd do better, I told myself, when I didn't see them every day. Less time together would change my perspective, I was sure.

"What did you want to talk about, *mijita*?" Mom walked past me as she spoke, stopping where she could see the front of the diner, watching for a late night customer. I heard the rattle of toys from the opposite direction and took up a post of my own, moving to where I could see both of them and still get to Ria in the office if she started to cry or throw a fit.

"What's going on?" Dad asked. He set aside his bottle of cleaning spray, leaning against the stove, giving me his full attention.

"I don't know how to say this to you but I . . ."

"Spit it out, Lucy. I've got a kitchen to clean." To anyone else, his words would have sounded forceful, short, or curt. That was how

Dad was though. There was gentle joking behind his gruff words. He played tough, but he was all heart.

"Dad, Mom, I quit."

My statement shocked them both, freezing them in silence. Cleaning up was forgotten. Late customers would have to wait. They focused on me, making me squirm with the intensity of their stares.

"You what?"

"I quit. I'm not going to work at the diner anymore."

"Is this because your father made you take time off last week?"

"No, Mami, it isn't. I'm doing something else with my life." I explained everything, unfolding the events of the last several days starting with the for sale sign and ending with the meeting with Miss Patsy and Sandie with an I and an E yesterday.

"You don't seem very excited about it, Luz. Are you sure this is what you want to do?" Dad asked.

"What do you know about this Carson?" Mom asked before I could answer Dad. "Is he trustworthy? He seems perfectly nice when he's in here and at church, but Luz, you don't know him. I've heard Joy's stories about him. He's a wanderer."

"Mom, he grew up in a B and B in New Orleans. He's better prepared for this than I am. Dad, I'm not sure of anything anymore. Well, I am sure of one thing. I'm sure I need a change. I can't keep going along in a rut like I have been since Teo passed. Something has to change. This sort of fell into my lap so I'm going with it." I paused and a thought flashed into my brain. I remembered talking to Teo the day before. "Maybe, just maybe, this is a God thing."

"Luz," Mom gasped, wrapping me in her arms. "You haven't said that since . . ." She choked up and hugged me tighter. We might not be pray-over-meals religious people, but God has always played a huge role in our family. I knew Mom had been waiting for me to use those two words again. *God things.* She'd been the one who taught me about them. We finally broke apart, tears in both our eyes, and looked at Dad.

For what felt like decades he simply stood there, arms crossed over his chest, staring at me with narrowed eyes. I could tell he was running it all through his businessman's brain. Would a bed and breakfast work in Rio Verde? Could his daughter run one? Would it be safe for a single mom to run a business built on inviting strangers into her home? Dad always thought fast so I knew the number of questions his brain was churning out was probably massive. Finally, though, he smiled.

"We'll help you where ever we can. I can't say I totally understand this, but I've never been where you are right now. I hope this is the right thing for you and Ria."

"Me too, Dad. Me too."

Chapter Twenty-Five

"I'm sorry. Say all that again. You did what?" Joy stared at me, a cookie halfway frozen on its journey to her mouth, her snack forgotten as my news sunk in.

"I bought the Tate House. With Carson. We're going into business together." My schedule for the day was now complete. I'd told Mom and Dad and now my friends. It was a relief to have it all in the open. Secrets drove me crazy. The moment I thought about secrets my inner voice came to life. *What about that skipped heartbeat? What about Carson?* I ignored it. That was a secret I wasn't ready to face yet.

"Miss Patsy's house? The one you talked about at Sunday lunch a while back? That house?"

I looked over at my friends. Mallie Jo. Joy. Isabel. Lane. We were on the roof of Joy's bakery, right across the town square from the diner. We could see most of the town from here. In fact, we could see the roof of the house in question. The house that would soon be my home. It was our spot, this roof. We had a row of folding chairs up here at all times, ready and waiting. It was our retreat. Where we went to talk about all the life stuff, the adult stuff, as Lane said. We'd planned Mallie's wedding up here. We'd watched Joy decide to stay in Rio Verde and slowly realize she was falling in love with Will. Later we'd planned her wedding, too. They'd spent hours up here crying with me when Teo had died. We'd plan Joy's baby shower soon. It was a great place to discuss the next event in our lives.

"Yeah, Isabel. That house. The only Tate House in town."

"Luz Selena Baca. Have you lost your mind? I thought you were joking the other day."

I sighed and looked down the row at my sister and rolled my eyes at her. She stuck out her tongue in return. I looked away, out at

Rio Verde's downtown. What little of it there was. The square in the center, before us, a grassy park, host to every city event. The Red, White, and Blue Diner. The bank. A hardware store just out of sight below us. A flower shop. An ice cream shop. On and on and on the list went. I would have to stop calling Rio Verde a small town soon. We were growing fast. I was happy about it but still . . . everywhere I looked I saw Mateo. No. Mateo's ghost. All the familiar things in my life were haunted by him.

"I need to do something new, Is. I needed something . . ." Sadness rushed into me, filling me up, stopping my words.

Like always, Mallie reacted first. She threw an arm across my shoulders and hugged me to her side, nearly tipping over both our chairs. Since everything had gone wrong I'd realized how lucky I was to have a friend like her.

"It'll be great, Lucy Lou."

"Hey, if I can run a bakery, Luz can do this. I didn't know anything about running a business when I started this. I learned. So will you." The jing-jingle of bells punctuated Joy's declaration.

I leaned over, looking down to see who had left the bakery below. Will, who'd helped Joy learn how to run a business. He glanced up, waving when he saw us in our perch. I knew Carson and I would be reaching out to him before long for help with the bed and breakfast. I knew how to run a diner. This would be new and scary and hard but I knew Will would help us. If he'd been handy I would have hugged him. Will was going to be a huge help.

"Here," Joy said, passing Mallie a basket of cookies. "Sugar always makes the world a bit better. You can do this. We'll help."

"She's right, Luz. You can do this. I know I haven't been part of this circle of friends for long but, girl, you're one of the toughest people I know. With everything you've dealt with over the last year, you can totally do this whole B and B thing." Lane added her support to Joy and Mallie's. I looked down the row again to my sister, waiting for her to share her thoughts.

"Well, sissy, have you told Mom and Dad?"

"Yup. This afternoon. Told them and quit the diner."

"Did you tell Grace?"

I rolled my eyes at her. Grace may be off at vet school but she's still my sister. "Yes, I called Grace and told her. Texted Marisol since she was in class. Texted Tres too. Our whole family knows." I'd had to tell them first. I loved my best friends but my siblings would have been furious if they'd found out last.

"Hmmm, okay." She went quiet and looked away from the square toward the tall trees and pitched roofs of the historic district. I knew she was looking at the roof the Tate House. "I think it's an awesome idea. We haven't had a bed and breakfast in town since The Prairie Cottages closed five, six years ago. I think it did really well until the owners got divorced."

"It did really well. I tried to get my folks a night there for their anniversary back when it was open. Saved all my allowance and even sold my iPod. Ended up not being able to get a room for them. The place was booked up for nearly a year," Lane said.

Joy reached over and squeezed her sister's hand. I wasn't the only one who'd had a tough year. Lane and Joy's dad had divorced Lane's mom. I forgot how young she was sometimes. At twenty-four, she was the youngest in our group. Unless Marisol joined in or Grace was in town. Lane had hoped she could somehow save her parents' marriage. She'd hoped for years and years. I was sure the night at the now-closed bed and breakfast had been one of her attempts to make her parents fall in love again. She and Joy had gotten very close when her parents had finally divorced. In the months since then, she'd seen her parents happy for the first time in years. Her mom had gotten a new job and started over fresh. Her dad, their dad, was no longer our grumpy local sheriff. Seeing his happiness had bonded Joy and Lane.

We were all quiet for a while, sitting there eating our cookies and sipping our drinks. Finally, Mallie broke the silence.

"This really deserves a proper celebration. Let's head over to Dot's and get some real food." She rose, Joy right behind her.

"Yes! The baby loves barbecue." Joy grinned and laid her hand over her tiny baby bump.

"So does Joy," Mallie said, giving Joy a playful push.

"Very true. Joy likes all the food."

I laughed and followed them toward the stairs leading down into the apartment above the bakery. As we crossed the roof Isabel caught me, linking her arm through mine.

"I'm proud of you, Luz. I'm glad you're trying something new, moving forward with your life. Teo would be happy for you."

Tears filled my eyes as her words sunk in. "You think so?"

"I know so."

Isabel's assurance lifted me up. It was what I'd needed to hear. I needed him to be happy for me as I carried on down here without him. Now I felt sure that he was.

Chapter Twenty-Six

"You're crazy."

"Thanks, big brother. I'm glad you stopped by tonight. I really appreciate your support."

Tres rolled his eyes at me and my sarcasm and looked away. We were at my house. My soon-to-be-old house. A for sale sign had been planted in the front yard earlier today while I'd been quitting the diner. Moving forward. I was focusing on that and only that. Forward. I was hoping if I kept focused and moving the days would slip past and I wouldn't feel the stupid ball of grief inside of me so painfully well.

"You've never done anything like this." Tres' statement pulled me out of my head and got me refocused.

"I know. You'd never run a farm before but you're doing it now."

He stretched out his long legs and crossed his feet. His boots were muddy and so were the cuffs of his jeans. His shirt had a new rip in it and I knew I'd see it soon. Mallie would notice it and bring it to me to repair. Probably with a few of her own shirts, too. Tres could grow food to feed the whole town. Mallie could restore everyone's houses. Neither one of them could sew on a button though.

"You look tired, Tres." I reached over and grabbed his hand, giving it a squeeze before getting up from my chair. He'd spent every day at the trial for a week. Then he'd worked in the dark each night, trying to stay on top of business. I was only seeing him tonight because he'd run to town for a tractor part. I laid my hand on his shoulder, pausing as I walked past. "Go home. Hug your wife. Get some sleep."

"I can't sleep. One of my sisters has gone crazy."

"I'm not crazy. I'm sad. I'm stuck. I have to do something new. Something to change the rut I'm in. Or I really will go crazy." I

114

paused, sighed. I was tired, too. Tired in lots of different ways. "I heard y'all talking about me. The night before Mallie's surgery. I heard y'all. I'm trying to get better, Tres. To do it I have to change my life. Leaving things the same will keep me stuck in this . . . this quicksand of sadness. I know y'all meant well that night, you always mean well, but hearing y'all talking about me as if I was broken really hurt. I guess I needed to hear it though, because I'm trying so much harder now."

Tres didn't say anything, although he did look embarrassed for a second. I knew my brother well and knew he was sorry I'd caught them talking about me. For a while he sat there, watching my neighborhood. Things were quiet for once. Normally there was always something going on. Kids playing. Someone working outside. Dogs barking. On Fridays, there was always at least one house having a party. Some nights I'd even hear a garage band practicing. It was a young neighborhood and always busy. I would miss it. Moving to the Tate House, though, would be like going home. It was only a few streets over from the one I'd grown up on. It would be nice to be closer to Mom and Dad again and to Mallie's dad Jonah. It would be nice to be surrounded by family again instead of being over here on my own.

"I'm worried about you, sister."

"I'm worried about you too, big brother." He needed to talk about Teo. I needed him to talk about it. He and I had been Teo's people and we'd both been grieving for him on our own. I wished I'd realized months ago how much I needed to talk about Teo. I'd been so afraid of burdening everyone with my grief that I hadn't given anyone else the space to share their grief with me.

We went quiet again, crickets and a distant neighborhood dog filling the space between our words.

"I miss him too," Tres finally said. I knew he did. It hurt my heart even more to know my brother was hurting too. Mateo had been Tres' best friend since they'd been kids. He stood and walked over, grabbing me in a rough bear hug. I wrapped my arms around his waist and hung on for a bit, not letting him walk away. No matter how old I got, a hug from my big brother would always be one of the most

115

comforting things in the world. Tres may have picked on me and even whooped my butt a time or two, but he also always had my back.

"I need you to think about something," Tres said, stepping away from me. He was serious, serious and worried. My big brother was a lot of things, but he was rarely so serious and worried. It made me instantly concerned.

"What, Tres?"

"Come to the trial with me tomorrow."

My heart stopped, clenched and frozen, missing several beats. The trial. I'd been hiding from it really well. Avoiding the news. Ignoring the local paper and the persistent editor who kept calling me for comment. Leaving the room when people started to talk about it. I'd even stopped listening to all to the local radio stations. I knew it was still dragging on—five days and counting. Carson and Tres both insisted on texting me a short report each day even though most didn't say much more than "still going on." I knew Tres was there every day and Joy usually managed to be there for at least an hour or so too. I'd decided they were representing me. I didn't need to go, I'd told myself. In reality, I was scared to go. Scared to come face to face with the man who had ruined my world.

"I don't think . . ."

"It's almost over."

"Really?" I thought of my phone, inside on the table. Had I missed Carson's nightly update? I tried to remember if I'd heard my text alert while at Dot's with the girls.

"Closing arguments tomorrow. Then it's all in the hands of the jury. Maybe you being there at the end will be the final push they need to convict him."

"You don't think they're already convinced?"

"I'm not sure. I just think seeing you would be good. I think they need to see the person who was most destroyed by what that guy did. I don't think you need to put on a show and cry or try to jump over the courtroom railing and strangle him. I think you just need to be there. They need to see that a person's life is hanging in the balance.

116

A good person who just wants to see justice done so she can move on with her life."

"Really?" I asked again. Somehow, knowing it was almost over made it a little less daunting.

"Really. One, maybe two more days left. I promise. I think you need to be there. For the end."

The end. A weight shifted on my shoulders, lightening. I could see it end, I told myself. For Mateo. For Ria. For me.

"Okay. I'll go with you."

He gave me another big hug, squeezing the air out of my lungs.

"Good. I'm going home. I'll see you tomorrow." He kissed the top of my head and then swatted me on the butt. "Go take care of my niece, Loca."

"I love you, Tres."

"Love you too, Lucy."

I watched until his truck had disappeared around the corner, then headed back into the house and to the mess I'd left waiting. When I'd seen the for sale sign today, I'd suddenly felt like I needed to move right now. Like I needed to pack up the whole house. Like I needed to be gone. I couldn't go anywhere yet though. Miss Patsy was still living in the Tate House, although she'd let us start working on removing the wallpaper. She'd move into her new condo at the senior village tomorrow, though, so I was eager to get moved in. To get started on the project.

Carson was eager, too. He'd helped me pack for a few hours this afternoon before I'd met up with the girls. He'd admitted that living with a married couple with a baby on the way wasn't exactly fun. We both were sitting on pause, balanced on an edge, waiting for this new part of our lives to finally start. There was so much to be done before we could officially open the bed and breakfast. We both had long lists of stuff to get done. I wanted to fast forward to a time when it was up and running and doing well.

Time had other plans, though, and was moving at a painfully slow and normal pace.

Time wouldn't let me skip the things I wanted to skip. Going to the trial was another hurdle between me and moving forward. Maybe with it over, with that man in prison, maybe then moving forward wouldn't be such a challenge.

Chapter Twenty-Seven

"What do you wear to court?" I spoke to my closet and to the cell phone balanced nearby in a shoe.

"Why do you sound all echo-y?" Mallie's voice filled the closet, louder than I was ready for so early in the morning. I winced and turned down the volume.

"I've got you on speaker and am standing in my closet. Now what do you wear to go to court?"

"Did my husband convince you to go with him?"

"He did."

I heard her sigh and say, "Tres, dang it." Then I heard him ask "What?" in a voice full of innocence. I guessed she'd told him to leave me alone about the trial and that he'd ignored her.

"Okay," Mallie said when she came back on the line. "Wear something comfortable because you'll be sitting a lot. Comfy shoes too, because when you aren't sitting, you'll be standing and all the floors in the courthouse are marble, and it kills your back after a while. That may just be Tres' problem though. He's a big baby."

I heard a crash and Mallie's voice got distant again. "Don't you be throwing stuff at me. I'm recovering from major surgery and I'm your wife. You promised to love and treasure me." I heard Tres start laughing then a door slam.

"Can I wear jeans?" I asked her. "Jeans and tennis shoes and a comfy sweater?"

"Sounds perfect."

"Good. Did Tres leave? Do I need to hurry?"

"He just walked out the door. He'll pick you up in a bit. I'd hurry."

119

I went quiet for a moment, listening to the sounds of Mallie hobbling around her kitchen, eating breakfast. I knew when she bumped her bulky knee brace on a cabinet by the whispered curse word. I knew when their two dogs crashed against the backdoor by the sudden pair of thuds, then the accompanying whines as they asked to come in the house. I could see her starting her day. I needed to start mine too, but I couldn't seem to leave my closet.

"Mal, what am I going to do with Ria? Should I take her?"

"Shoot. I didn't think of that. Drop her off at the bakery. Aunt Jo and I will come get her. She can go to physical therapy with me."

"Really? You want to take on your aunt, my toddler, and physical therapy all at once?"

"I've probably lost my mind but yeah, I'll take it on."

I told her she was crazy, then hung up the phone. As I picked out a sweater and grabbed some jeans I heard a thud from the hallway then Ria's whimpering cry. I couldn't help but think that my kid and Mallie's dogs sounded a lot alike first thing in the morning.

*****

I'd hidden from the trial so well that the amount of press at the courthouse shocked me. Neither Carson nor Tres had mentioned press coverage at all in their updates. Even the repeated phone calls from the local paper hadn't clued me in. There weren't TV vans from all over the US, but the attention was still big for the top of Texas. Three vans from the three local networks, plus a few cars bearing the names of a couple of local papers. Several police cars too with cops standing nearby, ready to keep things calm if they had to. Tres drove right past it all though, circling the courthouse then driving into the residential neighborhood behind it.

"I've been parking over here, going in the back. The first day the press darn near tackled anyone connected to Mateo. Thankfully the local cops have been making them stay up front so folks can come and go the back way."

I nodded and followed him through the street, past neat houses with tidy lawns and trees with a few fall-colored leaves still clinging to the branches. My brain kept trying to panic about the trial so I made myself focus on other things. November was passing by quickly. Thanksgiving and Christmas would be here soon. Distracting myself wasn't working, so I focused on Tres' back as he walked in front of me, watching him. I tried to focus on little details on the back of his jacket—spots of lint or the occasional dog hair. I didn't trust myself to talk to him, to make conversation. My hold on myself was too unsteady. Talking felt too scary. Like it would take my focus off my distraction attempts long enough to allow my emotions to shatter or explode or something. Tres led the way to the back of the building to a door with a guard posted beside it. The man nodded to him and opened the door for us. I was thankful the guard didn't try to start some small talk I would have been forced to respond to. The way I felt I probably would have burst into tears or turned and run back to the truck.

Tres kept walking, down a quiet hallway lined with closed doors. Up an empty staircase probably meant for courthouse employees only. At the third flight of stairs he stopped at a door, finally looking back at me.

"This is it. We're pretty early so we should be able to go in and take a seat before the crowd really starts to gather. Are you ready?"

"Yes, let's go." I heard myself say the words. Heard them echo in the stairwell up to the final floor above us. I wished I felt as brave as those words sounded.

I followed Tres into a brightly lit hallway. It was all shades of brown, a contrast to the cinder block stairwell and with the metal stairs. The public part of the courthouse was much warmer and inviting. Tan and white tile floors. Walls paneled in a deep, rich brown wood Mallie could have given me the name of. The walls were adorned with big oil paintings all featuring your typical west Texas scenes—cowboys gathering cattle, lone oil wells, distant groups of Native Americans, weathered houses and barns, sunrises, sunsets, and thunderstorms. In case someone forgot they were in Texas, the artwork would remind them. There were small groups of people scattered up and down the hallway. None looked up at our sudden appearance. Their hushed conversations were the only sounds.

"Come on," Tres said, heading toward a pair of tall, imposing wooden doors at the end of the hallway opposite us. Two uniformed officers stood on either side, one opening a door for us as we approached. The big courtroom was much like the hallway. Shades of brown and tan. Stone and wood. A couple more clusters of people in deep conversation. There were already several people scattered among the rows of benches before the big judge's bench. Some had newspapers out, others their cell phones, and one older lady had her knitting.

"She gave me a hat yesterday. She's giving them out every day," Tres whispered to me, leading the way to a seat near the front.

"I don't really want to sit up front, Tres."

"Trust me, sis, you do. You need to."

He didn't give me a choice, pushing me into a row, then closing off my escape route when he followed me. I relented and walked toward the other end, taking a seat against the wooden railing enclosing the gallery.

"That's her," he said suddenly, nodding his head behind us. "Over your right shoulder. Back row."

I didn't understand what he was talking about but looked behind me, trying to be casual. On the back row, close to the door, sat a young woman with a little girl a few years older than Ria. She looked like she was in her early twenties so she must have been a teen mom to have a kid around five years old. I still didn't know who she was though.

"Who is she?"

"The woman Teo saved. He stepped between her and her little girl."

I felt the color drain out of my face. My stomach sank and I glanced at her again. Several times over the past year I'd struggled

122

with hating her for being in the truck stop that night. For foolishly stepping into the line of sight of the gunman, trying to run for the door. I played the what-if-game in my head a lot, every scenario starring her. What if she hadn't been there? What if she'd hidden behind a shelf instead of trying to run? What if, what if, what if. Seeing her now, arm around her little girl, none of those thoughts mattered anymore. For the first time I could see that night through Teo's eyes. I understood why he'd done it. He'd seen a mother and child.

He'd seen me and Ria.

I didn't have time to dwell on the stranger and her child. Things started to happen in the courtroom quickly. I'd served on a jury once so I sort of knew what would happen. Court officers filed in, the court reporter took her seat at her little typewriter. The seats in the gallery filled up. It was fascinating to watch all the parts of a trial come together. I was thankful to see the press was kept out. I hoped to escape without ending up on the news or in the paper. I didn't want to be forever labeled the grieving widow or something similar. Soon the lawyers arrived in their fancy suits with their important-looking briefcases. We were seated behind the prosecutors. One of the trio of men was familiar.

"The middle guy is Mr. Coulter's partner, Shawn Dixon. I've only seen him a once or twice. Never spoken to him."

"Same here. He's only come into the diner a few times," I whispered back to Tres.

"Everyone does eventually."

"Good point," I conceded. Tres was right. Rio Verde didn't have a wealth of restaurants. Eventually, every resident had come, or would come, into the Red, White, and Blue. Mr. Dixon, though, was a rare sight in the diner. Or anywhere else in town. I'd spoken to him to take his order and given him his bill and nothing more. I'd heard about him though. Mr. Coulter had bragged about him when he'd joined the law firm. Apparently, he was something special in the legal world. I hoped his bragging hadn't been boasting. I hoped he and the two other men had done their job well.

The judge came in, taking her seat behind the bench, the courtroom going silent at her appearance. Last was the defendant. Him. It was the first time I'd seen him in the flesh. Jason Kurb. He shuffled in, wearing a suit and tie, handcuffed and flanked by burly guards. In my head, he was a monster. Larger than life. In reality, he was a small, squirrelly looking man. Stringy hair. Pale complexion. Pockmarked skin and hollow, sunken eyes. The suit hung on him, probably borrowed and at least two sizes too big. He looked weak. Like even Ria could have landed a solid punch and knocked him out.

He wasn't scary anymore. He was vile, evil, but not scary. As I watched him take his seat, I noticed a gleam of sweat on his forehead and upper lip. His hands, clutched together before him on the table, trembled violently. Tres noticed too and leaned over to me, explaining to me there was a rumor going around that was Kurb was a drug addict. He'd looked worse and worse as the trial wore on, Tres explained. Tres thought he'd been able to score drugs while he'd waited in jail for the trial to start but now was painfully detoxing as he'd sat in the small courthouse jail in the basement the past week. I wanted to hate this pitiful man before me but I found I couldn't. I felt sorry for him. I wondered how his life had gotten so far off track that he'd ended up in a truck stop with a gun.

"He's pathetic," I whispered to Tres.

"I know. I hate what he did but . . ."

"He looks like he's dying."

Tres nodded and started to speak but the judge banged the gavel, starting the court session.

Here we go.

Chapter Twenty-Eight

Guilty.

Guilty on all charges.

Second-degree murder.

There was still a sentence to be handed out tomorrow, but that one little word changed my world as much as his thoughtless violence had. He'd most likely spend the rest of his days behind bars.

Guilty.

A loss of freedom for Jason Kurb.

Regained freedom for me.

I replayed the events of the day as I laid in bed. The lawyers had ruled the day with their long speeches and the review of the evidence. First had come Mr. Dixon. He'd given me a nod before he'd stood and started talking. I got the feeling that he was about to sum up his case more for me than for the jury. Dixon had started with a review of the evidence against Kurb. Security footage from the truck stop. Testimony from all the witnesses. Gunshot residue on Kurb's hand. He ticked off everything ending with the bullets that had killed Teo—bullets that matched the gun Kurb had been in possession of when he'd been arrested that night. Then Dixon had gone over Kurb's crime spree that summer, including the robbery of Joy's bakery and the beating he'd given her. He summed everything up by talking about Kurb's history of drug abuse and violence. Then he'd surprised me and pointed me out to the jury.

"Mrs. Baca had her whole world torn apart by this man's senseless act. She now has to raise her child alone. I want each of you to put yourself in her shoes. Any one of us, myself included, could have lost someone to Kurb that day. Any one of us could have died at his hands."

That last part of his speech had taken my breath away. I understood what he was doing, playing to the emotions of the jury members. It still got to me, imagining the people I loved being in my place. Only Tres' whispered wisecrack had kept me from breaking down. "The guy is a genius," he'd said then added, "an evil genius. Thank God he's on our side."

After Dixon sat, the defense attorney had stood and taken his turn. It hadn't taken him nearly as long. As he reviewed his own case it was clear he didn't have much to stand on. He tried to lay blame on Kurb's poor childhood, his abusive father, his time spent in and out of jail. Then he blamed the drugs Kurb had been on and tried to claim that he'd been so high, so out of his mind, that he couldn't have known what he was really doing that night. By the time he sat down, I was starting to think even he didn't believe in his own case.

Then the jury was dismissed and the waiting began. Tres slipped out and got us a fast food lunch that we ate in the hallway outside along with several other people. The knitting lady gave me a pretty yellow hat. I'd expected the wait to take a while. Maybe even a day or two, but the jury had come back in two hours.

Two hours and one word and the hell of the past year was over.

Just.

Like.

That.

It had been hours and yet I still couldn't stop repeating that one word over and over in my head. I forced myself to refocus and reached for my phone and pulled up Tres' number.

I typed a message: *Tres, what do I do now? Now he's been found guilty. Now he is going to probably, hopefully, spend his life in prison.* I reread it and hit send.

A trio of little dots appeared on his side of the conversation and I smiled. Mallie had told me that he did crosswords on his phone before bed. Clearly, I'd interrupted his game to get his attention so quickly.

You do what you've started doing. You build a new life. You keep working on the bed and breakfast with Carson. You live life. His reply made me look away from the phone and take in my bedroom. I'd packed for a while when I'd gotten home.

I live life, I typed.

Yup. No more going through the motions.

I haven't been . . . I began, then hit send and started a second sentence. I didn't get it typed before he texted back.

Yes, you have. It's okay though. If I'd been in your shoes, I'd probably have been on autopilot this year too.

I thought about Teo, up in Heaven, keeping watch over all of us this past year. I'd felt him so often.

Thanksgiving is next week right?

A little over a week. I didn't have to see him to know he was giving me a look. His what-are-you-up-to look. I'd gotten it a lot in my life.

Good. Plenty of time, I typed.

Time for what? I could feel the suspicion coming through his text.

To host our whole huge family for Thanksgiving. At the Tate House.

You're insane. You don't even live there yet.

We're moving in tomorrow, I countered.

It's not enough time.

Sure it is. You're going to help me. Everyone will.

He didn't reply with words, just an eye-rolling emoji, but I knew he'd be there tomorrow, helping me move and he'd be there as much as possible every day until Thanksgiving.

*****

"Pizza always seems to taste best when you've worked hard all day."

I nodded in agreement, my mouth too full to speak.

127

"Pizza!" Ria yelled as she picked the pepperoni off her slice. She always deconstructed her pizza. All her food really. She even tried to take apart a peanut butter and jelly sandwich the other day. She'd scraped the jelly off onto her highchair tray and made a pile, then started on the peanut butter. I'd stopped her before she'd covered the whole chair and herself with peanut butter.

I looked around the guest house as I ate. Carson, Ria, and I were eating on the living room floor, surrounded by everything from my old house. Boxes. Furniture. Chaos. I'd watched it happen. I'd helped. I still didn't know how we'd managed to move an entire house in two days. There had been people helping that I didn't even know. All the furniture Miss Patsy had left behind had been crammed into the little garage when Isabel and I had gotten here with the first load. Ria and I would be living in this mess while I unpacked us and figured out what to do with all things in the garage.

Ria started to yawn so I put aside my food and hustled her off to bed. Her room was the only mess-free spot in the cottage. I'd made sure she had a familiar looking room to sleep in. My own bed was piled with all of my clothes and our sheets and towels. I'd probably end up sleeping on the couch. *Soon, too,* I thought as I yawned my way down the hallway.

"So how's it feel?" Carson asked.

"How does what feel?" I dropped back down to the floor and grabbed another slice of pizza.

"Your whole world changed in the past few days. You became a business owner. According to the news, the bad guy is going to be in prison forever. You spent two days moving. How does it all feel?"

"Overwhelming." I thought for a moment, reaching over and grabbing Carson's canned drink. I took a long drink and handed it back. We'd both lost our drinks a dozen times today during the move. We'd given up and started sharing. I guess it meant we were good friends now. "It's overwhelming but exciting. It's been a long time since I've been excited about anything."

"Good then." He leaned back against a stack of boxes with a sigh. For the first time all day he looked tired. He closed his eyes, rolled his shoulders, then yawned. I caught it and yawned too.

"How does it feel? You've got a home for the first time in a lot of years."

"It feels strange. I've been camping or couch surfing for so long. It is kinda wild to know I have a place to live that isn't my Jeep. I have an address now. What's our address?"

"138 Sixth Avenue."

"Excellent. I live on Sixth Avenue. Sixth Avenue in Rio Verde, Texas. I'm a Texan now."

"You're weird when you're tired."

"Joy has pointed it out many times. So has my sister and my mom."

I laughed at him until a yawn stopped me. I had to get up and get back to unpacking before I fell asleep over the pizza. A thought stopped me before I stood, a question I'd always wanted to ask Carson.

"Why didn't you make it for Joy's wedding, Carson?"

He sat up and opened his eyes but didn't look at me, focusing instead at a distant spot over my left shoulder. Some of the sadness I'd seen in him the night he told me about his wife settled over his face.

"I wanted to be there. Joy's my best friend. There was someone else who needed me more though." He finally looked at me. I felt sorry for bringing it up. He looked so sad and so sorry. "My wife's brother. He's an alcoholic, too. His family, my in-laws, asked me to come back to Seward. They were staging an intervention to try to get him into rehab. When he agreed to go, I felt like I should stay up there. Help out his family while he was getting clean. Then I stayed a while longer when he got out to help him get his feet under him. If I could have been in two places I would have. I would have rather been here for Joy."

"I'm sorry I brought it up. I didn't know. Joy didn't tell me."

"That shouldn't surprise you. You know her pretty well by now."

"True," I agreed. "She protects her people, even from her other people. I'm still sorry for making you talk about it."

He sighed and stood, grabbing the pizza box. "It's okay. I feel like I'll always have this . . . duty to them. She would have wanted me to help them out. So if they call I head up there."

"I get it. I'll be tied to my husband's family for the rest of my life even though they're currently not speaking to me and have moved away without telling me." I paused, realizing how very un-family-like that all sounded. I shook my head and refocused on my point. 'My mom told me when you get married, you're not just marrying a person, you're marrying their family too."

"My mom always said something similar."

"See, they programmed us to think like this."

"Our moms might be evil geniuses." He held up his hands, twirling an imaginary mustache.

"Okay, that's it. You need sleep. You officially sound like a little kid." Together we cleaned up our picnic. Carson stayed and helped me put away everything strung out on my bed before going over to his apartment in the main house. I knew he'd probably put half my things where I'd never find them, but I was grateful to be able to climb, exhausted, into my own bed.

Chapter Twenty-Nine

"That's enough of that."

I heard the voice, clear as day, inside my own head. It was my own voice, but not. I wiped the tears away and pushed myself off the floor, sitting up to look around the dark room.

Two o'clock. Ria was asleep, a quick glance at the baby monitor confirmed it. Only a light in the hallway was on. The rest of the house was totally dark. I'd woken up suddenly an hour earlier and knew I wouldn't go back to sleep. Moving had left me too wired. I'd come in here to resume unpacking and instead had a pity party. I'd cried myself out and was laying on the floor, staring up at the ceiling when the voice had sounded in my head.

"Enough of what?" I whispered the words to the dark, messy room. I hadn't even bothered with lights to work by. Light from the full moon and the streetlights filled the little kitchen with enough light to see. It was a false light though, a golden light I'd always thought seemed to promise a brightness it never delivered. I needed to turn on an actual light and really get to work. Or go back to bed.

In my head, a thought bloomed and grew. That was enough of the crying. Enough of the dwelling. Enough of the half-assing life. Enough of it all.

When Mateo died, I'd stopped believing in God things. I still believed in God but I'd stopped seeing His hand in everything. That part of my faith had been my compass most of my life. I'd been drifting without it. Blind to Him working in my life. Even though I'd somehow landed in the house of my dreams, landed a business partner, landed in a pile of goodness I hadn't dared to hope for.

"Well, it changes now," I said to the room. I stood and cleared myself a path through the mess I'd made before I'd broken down. I headed down the hall, away from the glow of the streetlights out front, detouring into Ria's room and checked on her. I crossed her room and looked out into the big backyard. Everything was dark in the big house across the yard, a gleam of frost on the grass and the gravel path between us. It was going to be a cold Thanksgiving the way the weather was headed. I was thankful Mallie had called a heating and cooling guy to come out and go over the systems at the Tate House before we'd moved in. It had been a happy surprise to discover everything was all in excellent working order.

I paused beside Maria's little bed, kissing her on the forehead. She didn't stir. Sound asleep. God had blessed me with such a good kid. She'd handled the past year with more grace than me. More grace than most people could have. She missed her dad. Asked about him a lot. We had all explained to her he was in Heaven with Jesus now. She accepted it without a second thought and now wanted to talk to him after we said her evening prayers. It was our new routine, pray and talk to Daddy. I looked forward to it as much as she did.

I was going to take a page from her book. Learn from the wisdom of a child. Stop dwelling on the things gone wrong and instead focus on the things going right. As I climbed into bed, I thought again of the voice that had jarred me out of my sulky pity party. I was sick of myself so I knew everyone else in my life was too. The conversation I'd overheard a few weeks back had confirmed it. I had to do more than change jobs and houses. I had to change the thinking pattern I'd fallen into. I had to stop linking everything back to my dead husband. It was a pit I'd fallen into. I had to start digging myself out of it.

I was going to start tonight with a decent night's sleep for once.

As I settled into bed, drifting toward sleep, the voice returned. Only a whisper this time, not a forceful command.

"That's better," it said. "Keep it up."

"I will," I said to the darkness, slipping into sleep.

*****

Sunday morning I woke to a blanket of frost on everything outside. The frost from two nights ago had returned, only this time it didn't retreat with the sunrise. Ria was fascinated by it so we went outside in our coats and pajamas to play. She delighted in the way her touch made the frost shrink and vanish. It made me excited to see her playing in the crunchy grass. Last winter she'd been too little to really understand the fun of snow. I had a good feeling this year would be different. More fun. Watching her discover the world made me see it with new eyes. She saw everything with such wonder.

She protested, loudly, when I made her come back inside. Once she realized we were headed to church though she got excited all over again.

"She's wound up today," I warned when I dropped her off. The volunteer, a new member named Holly, glanced behind her at the room full of rowdy toddlers.

"They all are," she said. "There's something in the air today."

I wished her luck and headed to my normal seat in the sanctuary. I wanted to get out of there before the children's minister saw me and tried to get me to stay and help. I loved my kid and I liked other kids but working with them was not my gift. I hadn't been able to convince him of that yet though.

I sat between Mallie and Joy, getting settled as the music started. We all stood, singing and praising until it was time for the next person to share their story. After Mallie kicked things off with her testimony last week I was excited to see what would come next. This Sunday a man near my own age took the stage. He introduced himself and set a bottle of water on the stool Mallie had sat on. For a second or two, I didn't hear what he said. I was focused on what he wore—a pair of denim shorts that would have been too cold for anyone else. Not for Danny Weir. He'd lost both legs to a suicide bomber in Iraq, he was explaining, black and metal prosthetic legs on display for all of us. I made myself focus on his words and was quickly fascinated by his testimony, which seemed to end too soon.

"I eventually realized I'd been given a second life," he said. "God had taken my old, shattered life, repackaged it, and given it back to me. It was filled with so many new blessings and promise and hope. I'm not thankful I lost my legs but I am thankful for the things God has done since I lost them. I know I wouldn't be who I am today if He hadn't walked beside me through everything that happened."

Dr. Bell took the stage, thanking Danny as everyone clapped. As the sanctuary settled he began to preach, expanding on everything Danny had shared.

I held onto Danny's final words the rest of the day. I realized he had experienced the same blessing Mallie had—beautiful, life-changing goodness in the wake of something truly terrible. All day I hoped and prayed I would come through my own loss and be able to say the same thing.

Chapter Thirty

"If I get to Heaven and the person who invented wallpaper is there, I'm going to request a transfer to Hell." I threw down the putty knife I'd been using, throwing the rag I'd held too. Then I kicked over my spray bottle for good measure. I wanted to stop my feet and storm out of the room but everyone was already staring at me.

"I'll second that," Carson said.

"Aren't y'all being a little extreme?" Mallie asked.

"No, no we aren't. Because you go home at night and so do you, Is. I stay here and once Ria is asleep I get the baby monitor and go back to work on all of this damned wallpaper. Carson and I both do." I turned my back on the wall I'd been working on. I couldn't stare at the mixture of dirty white plaster and dark purple floral paper anymore. "I'm going outside. I need a break."

I left before any of them could stop me. We'd been working nearly nonstop since in the four days since Carson and I had moved in, and we were still on the big dining room. I'd decided last night we'd have to open with wallpaper still in all the rooms upstairs. Maybe we could work on the second floor one room at a time when the place wasn't full of guests. Providing we could even get people to want to stay here. It was still packed full of furniture upholstered in fabric ranging from 1980s southwestern pastels to 1940s metallic florals. Miss Patsy hadn't taken anything but her bedroom furniture with her. She'd left all the other furniture and decor behind. As we worked on the house, the contents of the rooms got shuffled around, getting crammed into other rooms to be dealt with later. It was starting to look like a hoarder's house. Everything was well-made and fine, but not what Carson and I wanted to have in the house. It was daunting, all the stuff we needed to fix or replace or repaint. All the stuff we needed to sort into keep or sell piles. All. The. Stuff.

Right now, I would be happy to finish the damned dining room so we could have Thanksgiving dinner in there.

As I stormed through the house, I heard the buzz of power tools resume. My outburst had even stopped work on the kitchen. Mallie's crew was taking it apart so it could be refreshed and rearranged. I added it to my list of stresses. If the kitchen wasn't finished, I'd be cooking everything in the little kitchen in the guest house.

I slammed through the front screen door and made it to the top step of the porch before I sank down, exhausted. My anger had only carried me so far. I'd been pushing myself to the limit every day. Sitting down, emotionally drained, made me feel like an anchor was dragging me under. I shifted and laid back on the cold concrete porch. I needed to rest for a minute before I cracked completely. Maybe Tres was right; maybe trying to host Thanksgiving here was insane. I was probably putting too much pressure on myself but I just wanted to have Thanksgiving be the first holiday I celebrated in this house with all my family.

I heard a car pull up to the curb but I didn't move. I wanted to hold on to the tiny bit of rest I was getting as long as I possibly could. I tried to focus on the singing birds and ignore the approaching footsteps crunching through the fallen leaves scattered over the sidewalk, but it was impossible. Losing this little break made me even more frustrated and grumpy.

"Luz, you okay?" It was Joy. I reminded myself I loved Joy and that she usually came bearing baked goods.

"I'm okay. I needed a break from all. The. Wallpaper." I opened my eyes and sat up.

"I brought muffins," she said, holding out a little wicker basket.

The scent of fresh lemon hit me and I smiled. Lemon poppy seed. My favorite. I took them, not able to stop myself from breaking off a chunk of one and eating it with a smile.

"Thank you," I said over the mouthful of muffin.

"You're welcome. I also brought you help." She looked over her shoulder at the bakery van and the sliding door opened, her mom and Mallie's aunt Joann emerging. "They're banned from the bakery until they can stop treating me like a fragile invalid instead of a perfectly healthy pregnant woman."

The two women stepped around Joy and walked up the front steps. They both seemed a little afraid of my petite friend. She glared at them, shaking her head before walking off.

"What happened, ladies?" I looked up at them from the sidewalk, noting, not for the first time, how different the two were. Joann was every bit the preacher's wife. Prim and proper. Joy's mom, Susie, was more . . . rock and roll. Skinny jeans. Tattoos and an AA chip on a chain around her neck. The fact that the two were friends blew my mind all the time.

"We might have tried to do too much for her," Susie admitted.

"And told her to take it easy a few too many times," Joann added.

"Oh, I bet she yelled at you," I said as I walked up the stairs and into the house.

"She really did," Joann said. "Will has told me over and over she has a temper, but I've never seen it before."

I smiled and told them about the times I'd witnessed Joy's temper when I'd stopped by the bakery for breakfast. There was the time the milk delivery didn't show up one morning. Then another time the egg guy had shown up with only two dozen eggs. She'd made the poor man cry. I told them Joy always made me think of a line from *A Midsummer Night's Dream*: "Though she be but little, she is fierce." They both laughed and agreed. I gave them a quick tour of the house and ended in the dining room where the current wallpaper assault was still going on. Joann and Susie joined in right away, spray bottles and scrapers in hand. It was exhausting work but by the time we called it a day, the first room in the house was almost free of wallpaper and the Tate House was a tiny bit closer to being ready for guests.

*****

My volunteers in the wallpaper war worked their tails off the next day, freeing the whole big dining room from its purple prison. We wouldn't be able to paint it until after Thanksgiving but being rid of the wallpaper improved the look of the space immensely. It felt bigger and somehow grander. The details of the room stood out more without the distraction of the wallpaper. The moldings around the door, windows, and ceiling commanded attention. The windows seemed taller. I couldn't wait to see the room completely finished.

"It'll look amazing once we get some paint on the walls and refinished the floors," Carson spoke from the doorway. He'd moved all the tools to the next room on the list.

"Think it will be okay for Thanksgiving?"

"Totally. Everyone will be more interested in the food than how this room looks."

"Oh, you haven't spent enough time with my parents yet. Mom will care. She won't say anything though."

"Distract her with the kitchen. Moms love kitchens and it'll be finished by tomorrow."

I heard him leave and turned to follow him. He headed down the short hallway to the kitchen. Mallie's crew had been working double and triple overtime to finish it. I'd promised to cook them all a huge thank you dinner right after the holidays. It was worth it though. The kitchen was like a new room. There was a new floor, covered with tiles that looked like aged, white painted brick. The tiles were in a herringbone pattern, dressing up the kitchen. It was the floor the kitchen should have always had. Mallie had saved all the cabinets, giving them a fresh coat of dove gray paint and putting them back in a new, more functional layout. The countertops had gone in today—a snowy quartz I was in love with. It would eventually go in all the bathrooms, too, along with the same brick tile. Tomorrow we'd get appliances and then we could start cooking. We were cutting it close with Thanksgiving only three days away, but we'd make it. Carson had already promised to help cook. Joy was, of course, bringing multiple desserts. Everyone was helping somehow. Isabel was even cleaning up the long dining room table Miss Patsy had left at the house. She'd recovered all the chairs with a fresh, durable deep blue fabric Carson had picked out. I'd been unsure until I'd seen it on one of the light oak chairs. It changed the 1980's era dining set into something more fitting for the new vision for the Tate House.

"You ready for your first Rio Verde holiday?" I asked Carson as I boosted myself up on the kitchen island.

"Your people don't scare me. You should be glad I talked my mom and sister out of coming up."

"They're two people. I'm from a family of five kids, the child of parents each with three siblings who all had multiple kids. When I was a kid, all my aunts and uncles lived close enough to descend upon Rio Verde for the holidays. My folks would put up tents outside for the kids if it was warm enough. The house couldn't even begin to hold everyone. It was insane. I miss having them all close, but the holidays are less stressful without twenty to thirty family members filling Mom and Dad's house."

He laughed, coming to stand across from me. "Okay, that does sound kind of terrifying."

"Mallie lived across the alley from me. I'd sneak over there to hide from my family all the time."

"I'd do the same thing but to hide from my grandmother and my mom. They fought a lot. Loudly."

"So just you, your sister, your mom, and your grandmother?" He nodded. "I can't imagine growing up in a family so small."

"It was nice most of the time. My dad wasn't in the picture, so it was the four of us most of the time. Five of us when Mom's dad and step mother would come over." He slid down the cabinets to the floor, sighing as he stretched his legs out on the floor. "My sister, Chloe, and I are only a year apart. She was always my shadow until she got into singing at school. She still sings with a little band a couple of times a month. She'd do more but Mom needs her help at the Osprey."

We sat in the kitchen talking until headlights flashed into the room, lighting up everything for a brief second. My dad, bringing Ria home. Carson and I both forced ourselves into motion reluctantly. The break and the quiet had been nice but too brief. We'd get a bit longer to eat dinner over in the guest house, then I'd put Ria to bed and would go to work on the wallpaper over there. I knew Carson did the same once he headed back to the big house for the night. I'd see lights on over there most evenings as he worked late too. I really hoped all our hard work would turn this old house into a successful business.

Chapter Thirty-One

When Dad brought Ria home, he demanded a tour of the house. It was the first time he'd asked to see it. The first time he had shown much interest in my new business venture. He and Mom had been willing to watch Ria for me a bit each day while I worked, but other than that they'd been distant since I quit working at the RWB. They had done the same thing to Tres when he had quit to farm and to Grace when she'd said she was going to vet school. Even to Isabel when she'd partnered with Mallie and her dad to offer decorating services to their renovation clients. Each time they'd stepped back and kept watch while their children worked to find their own way in the world. It was sort of frustrating to be on the receiving end of it for the first time. I would have rather had them cheering me on. The watching and waiting made me uneasy.

Marisol was their golden child right now. Since she had finished high school she had gotten serious about learning the restaurant business. She was taking classes online at the local community college. She was determined to make the family proud one day. I knew Mom and Dad were proud of all their kids but they had a hard time with so many of us walking away from the diner.

So it was a pretty big deal to get to walk him around the Tate House and talk to him about the plans Carson and I had made. I showed him the library, telling him it had become my favorite room in the house. I told him about our idea to add comfy chairs and couches and to turn it into a kind of peaceful oasis. I walked him through the upstairs rooms and had to smile as he checked random things in each room. The lights in one. A window in another. The water pressure in each of the bathrooms. It was such a dad thing to do. When I took him down the back staircase to the kitchen, he went to town. Kitchens were his world. He checked over everything, opening doors, checking the sink, looking over the waiting connections for the stove, oven, dishwasher, and fridge.

"What do you think, Papi?"

"I think you and your friend are going to turn this big old house into a wonderful business. I think you'll have to work hard and I think it will be a struggle, but I think you can do it."

It was the best endorsement of this crazy new project anyone had ever given to me. I didn't say a word, just crossed the kitchen to hug him hard. He wrapped me in his arms and held on to me. I felt some of his strength and some of his faith in me flow into me, and I knew he was right. I could do it. I *would* do it.

"You've got to get rid of all the ugly wallpaper though." His laugh flowed into me too, getting me going. When he left, I felt more confident about this new life than I ever had. After I'd gotten Ria into bed that night, I went to work on the wallpaper in the guest house without all the anger I'd felt on other nights. I knew everything would be fine. My dad had said it would.

*****

The kitchen was done by lunch the next day. I wanted to dive right into cooking Thanksgiving dinner, but Mallie reminded me of one of my favorite Rio Verde traditions—the annual Thanksgiving festival. Granted, we had festivals and carnivals for nearly every holiday on the calendar, but the Thanksgiving one was always extra special. Lots of pies and other treats to sample. Retail booths filled with fall scented candles, wreaths, even quilts and pilgrim costumes. A celebration of my favorite time of year. I knew I'd have to get up way too early the next morning to get all the food cooked but going to the festival would be worth it.

142

"So this is a Thanksgiving carnival," Carson said as we got close to the center of town. We'd bundled up ourselves, then convinced Ria to wear her pink coat with the unicorn on it and walked the three blocks to the town square.

"No, this is a Thanksgiving festival. Now, around Christmas, we'll have a carnival. You'll like it too."

"Does this town celebrate everything?"

"Pretty much," I said, joining the crowd milling around the square. For a second I lost Carson, then he appeared at my side again. I was surprised when he reached out for Ria.

"I'll carry her and follow you. You give me the big tour."

I handed my heavy toddler over without a second thought. She had no trouble walking around but she would whine to be carried. I was always happy to let someone else share the job. Plus, Ria was over the moon about Carson. She was good for him every time.

I led the way through the crowd, pointing out the best booths like the ladies from the Catholic church, who made the most delicious pecan pie in the world and the local quilting society, who made quilts all year to sell at this festival each fall. Word about our plans for the Tate House had spread so we got stopped a lot and spent more time fielding questions than we did checking out the booths. We were still able to get samples of pie and fudge and cookies and a big cup of apple cider to share. I didn't buy a thing this year, but it was still great fun to wander around, showing it all to Carson.

Darkness fell quickly and with it, the musical part of the event started. As the band started to play, Carson and I took the now cranky Ria and slipped away, heading home. As we headed back, a thought struck me. We looked like a family. A family heading home with a tired kid. The thought rattled me. I'd been part of a family. I'd had that life. I liked Carson more than a little. He was quickly becoming my favorite person in fact, but I wasn't sure I was ready to start thinking of him in any other ways than as a friend. My heart skipped a single beat when I glanced over at him, as it was starting to do often. He carried my sleeping daughter as if she were his own. She had fallen asleep in his arms as if he were her dad. My heart skipped a beat again. I wondered why it kept doing that.

As we walked up the driveway to the house, Carson turned toward the cottage, heading right inside and directly to Ria's room. He knew what to do. He'd put her to bed before. When she didn't stay with Mom and Dad at the diner, she often played in whatever room we were working on, crashing when she ran out of steam. He'd brought her over here several times and put her to bed for me while I cleaned wallpaper glue off myself.

I heard Tres' voice in my head as I told Carson good night and watched him walk across the backyard.

You live life.

I guessed living life meant opening up your life to something— someone—new. I hadn't really thought of moving on, falling in love again. I also hadn't thought I'd mourn Teo for the rest of my life, staying a widow forever. That night, instead of working on little renovations around the guest house, instead of planning out the meal for tomorrow, I went straight to bed. Straight to bed to pray for guidance and understanding for the things heading my way.

Chapter Thirty-Two

"Luz, let me help."

"I think we've got it, Joy," I said, without any conviction, as I stepped around her searching for the roll of foil I'd had a second ago. "Carson, where is the . . ."

"Foil? Here." He handed it to me over Joy's head, quickly returning to the dish of sweet potatoes he was covering with tiny marshmallows. He handed Joy the last of the marshmallows when he finished and shoved her out of the kitchen.

"Go round everyone up," I told her. She headed off, eating marshmallows as she started calling out names. Dinner was almost ready. I covered the stuffing with foil and stopped and looked around the kitchen. There was food everywhere. The island held all the deserts Joy and my mom had brought. The countertops held all the food Carson and I had cooked. I'd gotten up at two this morning to start cooking. He'd gotten up with me and we'd worked side by side all day.

"You did good, Luz."

"*We* did good, Carson. This is a great inauguration for the new kitchen."

He nodded and yawned. "Can we give them the food and go take a nap?"

I caught his yawn and leaned back against the counter, suddenly deeply aware of how tired I was. "Wouldn't that be nice? We'll catch a nap after lunch."

"Don't kid yourself, sis," Tres said from the kitchen doorway. "You know Thanksgiving is an all-day affair in this family. After lunch comes board games and touch football, Carson. No naps for either of you." He circled the kitchen as he spoke, grabbing bites of food where he could. When he got close to me I smacked his hand away from the turkey.

"Carry some food to the dining room and stop sampling everything."

Tres picked up the turkey, grinning at Carson. "She's so bossy, my sister."

"I've noticed."

I glared at both of them. "Food. Dining room. Go. Both of you." I followed them, balancing a casserole dish in one hand, stuffing a handful of serving spoons in the back pocket of my jeans, and grabbing a pitcher of tea. Isabel and Marisol appeared, taking everything I'd been carrying, giving me a chance to go back for more stuff. I got to the doorway again and Grace appeared in the doorway, taking everything from me again. I watched her for a second, Mallie's cousin Kevin following her, helping her. I'd never have put the two of them together but being away at college had changed them both. Kevin had come back and worked for Mallie and her dad now. Grace was one year into vet school. They were still together in their unique, undefined relationship. They were together but didn't call each other boyfriend or girlfriend. They had made no plans for the future. Yet when they were in the same room, you could see they were both in it for the long haul. I caught Is laughing with Joy and wished she could find someone, too. Isabel seemed content to go it alone though. She'd always been the most independent of all of us and she was happy so nothing else mattered.

"Luz," Mom said, coming to stand beside me. "Can I do anything?"

"I think we've got it all, Mom." I glanced over my shoulder, checking the kitchen. All the desserts were still in there, where they would wait, but the main countertop was free of all the food for lunch.

"This is a beautiful thing you did for your family, *mijita*." She slipped her arm around my waist and guided me to the long table. Everyone started taking seats, Dad tucking Ria into a high chair between him and Mom. I sat between Carson and Joy. As soon as I sat, Mallie's dad Jonah stood at the head of the table and prayed over our meal. It was the most right my world had felt in a year. The most peaceful and happy I'd been since I lost Teo.

*****

It was amazing, really, how quickly nearly twenty people could eat food that had taken two people nearly eight hours to prepare. As soon as Tio Jonah said *amen*, everyone sort of went crazy. Casseroles were passed around, baskets of rolls too. The turkey was carved, drinks were poured. Everyone talked and ate and refilled plates and laughed and ate some more. After eating, Mom, Joann, and Susie kicked Carson and me out of the kitchen, promising to clean up everything while we went outside with everyone else.

Outside, the unseasonably warm day was perfect. Tres quickly marshaled everyone together for a touch football game. Ria wanted to play too and spent the game being carried around by Tres, then Will, then Carson, then Kevin. The guys carried the laughing toddler in one hand while ducking and dodging around in the backyard. I should have been worried about her but I knew each of the men would risk their own safety to keep her from being harmed. After football came dessert, brought outside by the moms. We all sat around in the yard and on the back porch eating more, talking more, hanging on to the wonderfulness of the day. Eventually, it was only Mallie, Joy, and me outside under a tree, getting cold as evening approached but still unwilling to go inside.

"This was a really great day," Joy said. She rested her hand on her growing baby bump. "We need to repeat it next year when this one is here."

Mallie reached over and touched Joy's bump. "I'm excited to meet this kid. He or she will make next Thanksgiving even more awesome."

"I don't know, y'all. What if the place is full of guests?" I said.

"We'll invite them, too. The more the merrier," Joy said.

"Things could be super different next year," I said. "Joy will be a mom."

"I'm betting Kevin will have popped the question to your sis," Mallie added.

"I think my folks will finally get together," Joy said. "They keep having lunch together. Like every day."

"It's about time."

"I know, right?"

"What does Lane think?" I asked.

"She's okay, I think. She seems happy to see Dad happy. Her mom started dating again so it's okay. She's gotten to a place where she's at peace with everything. She said they're both happier than they've been in a long time."

Mallie and Joy both went quiet, Mallie yawning and stretching. Joy closed her eyes, a sleepy smile on her face. I could hear laughing coming from the house as everyone hung out inside. I guessed that a jigsaw puzzle had appeared or possibly a board game. They were all probably gathered around the big table still. Everyone had tried to spread out in the living room after we ate but they all quickly decided all the antique furniture needed to go. Everyone had immediately pointed out what I'd known from the start. It was all terribly uncomfortable. I was glad Isabel was already pricing it for us. Other than the furniture, they'd all loved the house and the day. My brain reviewed everything, checking off all the good things until I circled back around to laying under a tree with my two best friends.

"Y'all, I think I might be ready to start dating again."

"What?"

"Say again?" Joy sat up and stared down at me. I glanced to my left and saw Mallie had done the same thing.

"Yeah. I got to thinking the other day. Teo wouldn't want me to be frozen like this. I don't want to be either. I never thought I'd be widowed so young or ever, but I also never thought I'd be the kind of woman who spends her whole life mourning."

Mallie pulled me up and hugged me. "Oh, that makes me so happy, Luz. You're so not meant to be alone."

"I know someone who will be happy to hear this news," Joy said, giving me a hug, too.

"What? Who?"

"Your business partner."

"No, really?" The thought had been in the back of my head for a while but hearing Joy say it out loud made it real. It was nice to know I hadn't been imagining things. Joy had noticed it, too.

As if talking about him had somehow called him, Carson appeared on the back porch. "Come on in, you three. Time for leftovers and more dessert."

The lure of more food got us all up and heading inside. I watched Carson more closely as we gathered around the table one more time. Was Joy right? Was there something there with him? Suddenly there was more for me to worry over than turning this house into a business.

*****

"I'm sorry I haven't been by," I said as I sat in the dry grass over Mateo's grave. It crunched beneath me as I got settled. I'd be covered in bits of crushed grass by the time I left but it didn't matter. I needed to talk to my husband. Darkness had settled over the empty cemetery. I'd had to hop the fence to get in—no one in their right mind would be visiting dead family at nearly midnight on Thanksgiving. I'd needed to be here though. Ria was sound asleep. Carson had promised to stay with her and I'd left him on my couch watching a movie. He'd understood why I'd had to come.

"Happy Thanksgiving, Babe. We missed you today." I paused, watching a car drive past. They didn't stop but I was glad I'd left my car off the street at the rear gate. I didn't want company.

"I got the Tate House. We got it, I mean. Carson and me. The house is amazing. Mallie has taken charge of rehabbing it. I'm so

149

excited to see it finished. Carson and I have been working our tails off, doing as much of the reno work we can."

I thought about what Joy had told me earlier. I'd watched Carson closely the rest of the day, and I'd caught him watching me on the sly a lot. It made my heart skip a couple of beats every single time.

"I like him. Carson. In more than a friendly way. I wasn't looking for it, but it seems as though my heart has other ideas. I want you to know I still love you. I always will. But I need to move my life forward, without you, because you're not coming back." My eyes filled with tears and I leaned forward, putting my head in my hands. I hadn't said those words out loud before. They hurt more than I thought they would.

"I will never stop missing you, Mateo. Never. But I have to leave you behind me. No, I have to leave *us* behind me."

For a while I sat there, watching the wind toss leaves around the tombstones. It was just me and the dead. Me and the dead. I didn't like it.

"I don't think I'll be coming to visit as much anymore. You're not really here anyway. I need to be in the world more. Spend less time here."

I stood, brushing grass off my seat. I touched his stone, dusting a few leaves off the top.

"I love you, Teo," I said then turned to go. I knew I wouldn't be back for a long time. I felt it in my heart. I'd finally, properly, told Mateo goodbye.

Chapter Thirty-Three

"Let's have dinner tonight." I blurted out the question in a rush before I could chicken out.

Carson glanced up at me from his spot on the floor. He had a pile of soggy wallpaper at his knees and some more stuck to his baseball cap. The little girl deep inside of me whispered he was adorable. The grown woman part of me was embarrassed by this sudden statement but then agreed. He went back to scraping wallpaper away from the hallway wainscoting before he answered me.

"We have dinner together almost every night. And breakfast. And lunch."

"I don't mean dinner like that. I mean dinner out. In clothes free from wallpaper glue and dust and dirt." I paused, letting Ria's sudden scream die out. "A dinner where Screamy the Wonderkid isn't invited."

"Like a date."

"I guess so, yeah."

He stared up at me. "You're terrible at this."

"I know." I felt myself flush and tried to will myself to be cool. I'd been married. I had a kid. I could handle asking a guy out on a date.

"How about I handle the asking out from now on?"

"From now on?"

"Yup."

I told myself, again, to be cool but my heart skipped a few beats anyway. "Is that a yes?"

"Yes. Dinner would be great."

Work flew by the rest of the day. Carson and I knocked out the front hallway in record time. Mallie's crew got the whole dining room painted. It was a good day. The kind of day that made me optimistic about the timeline for the project. The quick day also meant date night got here faster than I was ready for. Before I knew it Joy was letting herself in my front door, right on time to help me get ready and to watch Ria for me.

"Joy, thanks for coming over. And for staying with the kid tonight. Sorry to ask you so last minute."

"Hey, this is what friends are for. Besides, you can pay me back before long. Plus, I love Ria."

"You may change your mind after a night with her." Right on cue, she screamed, then resumed playing with her toys in her playpen. "She's rediscovered screaming since Thanksgiving. All day she's been driving Carson and me nuts. Random screams that scare the crap out of us. Even Mallie's crew is getting stressed out by it. If you can convince her to stop like you did last time, I'll make dinner for you and Will for a week."

"Oh, challenge accepted," she said, going to pick up Ria. I knew she wouldn't have a bit of trouble with her. Ria loved Joy and always had fun with her. I still hoped Joy would work some of her magic and get her past the screaming phase for good. Maybe she could work some magic on me to chase away the butterflies in my stomach.

I stared at myself in the bathroom mirror. My hair was too short to do much with but it looked good in the sleek bob instead of my normal messy, when-did-I-last-brush-it style. It felt good to be in something other than jeans and a t-shirt too, even though it felt strange to be in an actual dress for once.

"Are you sure this dress looks okay?"

"Maxi dresses look great on you," she said, appearing behind me in the mirror. Joy handed me a red cardigan. "Wear this. It's cold out tonight."

I did as she said and put it on. It worked well with the navy blue dress.

"Why am I so stinking nervous? I spend all day with him."

"Because you like him and it's exciting."

"It is. It's scary too, Joy. You don't think Teo is up in Heaven mad at me do you?"

Joy stepped up beside me and gave me a one-armed hug. "Not even a little bit. I think he's happy you're living your life again. He knows you still love him and always will. He also knows what we all know—your heart is big enough to love someone else one day too."

"Dang it, Joy," I said, pushing away a tear. "You're gonna ruin my makeup."

There was a sudden, loud knock from the side door of the cottage.

"Your date is here."

"Oh, *dios mio*. Okay. Here are my car keys. Use it if you want to go somewhere rather than move the car seat. I apologize in advance for all the screams she's sure to give you." I hugged her, kissed Ria, and grabbed my purse, rushing to the door. "Wish me luck."

"You're going to have a great time. Now go."

"Thanks, Joy. Love you."

"Love you too," she called out as I stepped outside, almost crashing right into Carson.

We both recovered from the collision and laughed.

"Shall we," Carson asked, offering me his arm. I linked mine with his, letting him lead the way. The nerves I'd felt inside vanished as we walked down the little gravel path to the driveway. Joy was right. This was going to be great.

*****

I was worried two people who spend almost every moment of every day working side by side wouldn't have anything to talk about on a date. I was wrong. We talked about everything. Favorite movies. Favorite books. Music. Church. Family. Ideas for the bed and breakfast. How Carson was handling life in one place. Why I'd never traveled and wandered like he had.

153

"I never wanted to," I explained. "Grace always wanted to be a vet. Tres always wanted to be a farmer. Marisol always wanted to run the diner. Isabel and I are the ones who always wanted to stay home. Isabel is kind of like Mallie. She likes making houses into homes and breathing life back into old things. She's talented and could go to a bigger city and do well, I'm sure, but she's happy here. She's home. Same for me. I wanted a family and a nice quiet life. Things sort of went wrong there, but I feel like maybe I'm back on my path again."

I ran out of steam and took a long drink of water. I watched Carson across the table. He was picking at the last of his dinner, lingering over one of the garlic knots, dipping it in the remains of his pasta sauce. He looked handsome tonight. He was always easy to look at, but all cleaned up and without a baseball cap—he looked good. It wasn't just that he was a handsome guy though. I could sit here and talk to him all night. I'd always been pretty stingy with my words. Working most of my life in a diner where I spent all day repeating the same idle chit-chat had always worn out my desire to talk. I didn't have that problem now. Being away from the diner and around someone I found fascinating made me want to sit and visit all the time.

"So why didn't you stay put? Why'd you leave New Orleans so young?"

"I was restless. I loved life down there. Even though I grew up there though, it never felt like home. I always had this . . . spinning compass inside of me, pushing me to move. It was like I had to follow it to the place that would feel like home."

"And now?" I was worried about what he'd say. I didn't want to lose my business partner. Or whatever else he might become.

"I feel settled. The compass has stopped spinning. Once I met Joy, I kind of knew I'd probably land near her. She's always been like an anchor for me."

"Was there ever anything more between y'all?" I had to ask. I felt like a moron the minute I said it but I had to ask.

"No way. She's my best friend. My mom met her once and she said we're two sides of the same coin. We'll always be connected but we'd kill each other if we tried to make our friendship something more. Besides, you hike the Appalachian Trail with someone, take as long as it took us, you get to a level of comfort with each other that wrecks any romantic ideas."

"I don't know, I saw the picture you took of her under the dogwood tree."

"It's just a picture. I needed a person in it to balance it. She was the only one I had handy." He grinned at me, open and honest. I'd seen their friendship right away. Once he'd settled here to stay the level of love and respect they had for each other was obvious. It still felt good to hear him say it.

"Why haven't I seen you taking pictures since you got here? Joy always said you were a photographer. You've only gotten you camera out one time that I've seen."

"Oh, I've been sneaking in photography time when I can. Someone has been working me to the ground in her battle against all things wallpaper."

I burst out laughing. He was right. Other than Thanksgiving Day, we'd been tearing down wallpaper nonstop. I was sick of it.

"Maybe we should take on another project for a while."

"Great idea. I see wallpaper every time I close my eyes."

We started brainstorming other projects to tackle until the hovering waiter finally got his point across. We needed to free up his table. As Carson drove us home, we picked up our conversation again and finally decided to organize the library as a way of a break. By the time he walked me back to my side door, I was confident the date had been a success. The gentlemanly kiss on my cheek had solidified it. Once I'd chased Joy out of the house and checked on a sleeping Ria, I laid in bed, wondering what I'd been so nervous about a few hours ago.

Chapter Thirty-Four

"No."

"Yes."

"No."

"Come on Luz, bend."

"No."

"What are y'all arguing about?" Mallie asked.

I looked over my shoulder at her, smiled hello, and turned back to Carson and gave him a good glare.

"Someone is being stubborn," Carson said, returning my glare.

I ignored both of them and looked around the library. Carson and I had been working in here for a couple of hours and the place was trashed. The floor-to-ceiling bookcases were all empty, stacks of books scattered all over the room. Ria was sacked out in her playpen in the middle of it all, empty juice box beside her. She looked like a little drunk passed out in the middle of a disaster area.

"It couldn't be Luz. She's never stubborn."

"I'm not being stubborn. I'm right. He's wrong."

"Oh, I'm not touching that. I'm going back to painting. Good luck, Carson."

"Thanks."

"This isn't working," I told him. "We need a new system."

"I can agree with that." He sat down on what Isabel had called a fainting couch. It looked tiny and fragile with a grown man sitting on it.

"We can't keep all of these books." I touched a stack with a toe of my tennis shoe. "No one will want to read all of these stuffy research books. Or all the medical textbooks. Or the legal textbooks." I pointed at the stacks as I spoke. We'd sorted them by topic and realized most of the topics were deeply boring.

"We'll put them up high. They'll look cool."

"No, they won't. They'll be clutter. We need fiction. Lots of fiction. Stuff people will want to read on vacation."

"We can't afford to restock this whole room with fiction. We'll keep everything, put the dry stuff up high, and slowly add more readable stuff over time."

"No."

"Yes."

"Oh, *dios mio*, you are not the boss of me."

"And you're not the boss of me."

"Ugh. Fine. How about this? I'll do some checking and see if I can get my hands on some cheap fiction and see if I can sell the boring books."

He narrowed his eyes and studied me. It was the first time we'd butted heads on business. As it turns out, neither of us liked to bend when we thought we were right. It was going to make business interesting. We'd probably need to hire a mediator. Maybe I could get Isabel to do the job. Pay her in tiny antique furniture.

"Yeah, okay. See what you can do. I'm going to go strip wallpaper. It's less frustrating than this library."

I fought the urge to call him a grumpy bear. He was already mad at me; I didn't want to make it worse. I smiled when he stalked past the library a few minutes later, armed with a scraper and a spray bottle. I wanted to call out to him, tell him he was cute when he was mad. I stopped myself again. *Don't poke the bear*, I told myself.

"The wallpaper better watch out," I said to my sleeping kid. She didn't budge. I retrieved my cell from one of the bookcases and went to sit in the window seat. I looked outside for a second, taking in the chilly day. December started tomorrow. Our weather seemed to be preparing for winter. It had been cold and dreary for days. I wanted it to snow. I loved snow. This place would look gorgeous surrounded by several fluffy inches of the white stuff. *Stop daydreaming* I said to myself, looking down at my phone. I pulled up Isabel's number and punched the call button.

"Is, are you free now? We need to get this house decluttered. It's officially getting in the way. Also, I need books for the library."

*****

Less than a week later, most of the Tate House was empty at last. Isabel put her all into selling the antique furniture. As it turned out, Mallie and her dad were restoring an old Victorian house in the next town. The owner ended up driving over and buying half of the furniture on the spot. Is had also found a bookstore going out of business up in Oklahoma. I managed to get several dozen paperbacks for nearly nothing, which meant I won the battle of the library with Carson. He got grumpy about it but packed up all the boring books anyway.

Work on the house was moving forward at a break-neck speed. Carson and I kept knocking out room after room, freeing more and more of the place from wallpaper. As soon as we'd finish a room, Mallie would put a couple of industrial fans in it to dry out the plaster. Then her crew took over. They'd also demoed the little downstairs powder room and were starting to put it back together.

It was time to start talking about the running-the-business stuff. Which I kept telling Carson over dinner on our second official date.

"But we need a proper name for the place and rates and a menu. What about events? We could rent the whole place out for events during the offseason. What even is our offseason?"

"Luz, can we please be two people out on a date? We'll talk business stuff tomorrow. We'll sit down, make a list, and get to work. We can even call my mom and get advice from her on anything you want."

I knew I was wearing him out. I couldn't seem to turn off the obsessive part of my brain. I felt bad. I was being a terrible date.

"I'm sorry. I'm ruining our night."

158

"No, you're not, but this place is not a repeat." He looked around the restaurant, frowning at the nearly empty space. "The food is okay at best and I haven't seen our waitress in twenty minutes. Let's get out of here." He pulled cash out of his wallet, guessed at our bill's total, then stood, offering me his hand.

"Where are we going to go now?"

"Let's swing by Sonic, get milkshakes, and go to our spot?"

"We have a spot now?"

"Yes, we do. Come on."

As it turned out, we did have a spot. Carson got lost trying to find it again but by then I realized where he was headed, so I directed him until we found the bluff over the city. It was too cold to sit outside and enjoy our milkshakes so we sat in the Jeep. The change of scenery was what my brain needed. All thoughts of the project were forgotten.

"Do you think . . ." Carson started. His voice trailed off and I looked over. His eyes followed a pair of headlights down the hill from us. They turned at a road we'd bypassed and eventually vanished.

"Do I think what?"

"Do you think they're up there, in Heaven, watching us?"

I knew who he was talking about. I'd wondered the same thing.

"What was her name? Your wife?"

"Lena."

"Lena. I like that name. Yeah, I bet they are. Mateo never met a stranger. They're probably friends."

"You think?"

"I do." We both went quiet again; the only sound was the both of us slurping up our milkshakes.

"What a date," I finally said. "I spend all of dinner talking about menus and room rates. We get dessert and you start talking about our dead spouses."

Carson burst out laughing. "We're a pair."

"We're awful at this whole dating thing."

"I used to be better, I swear. All romantic and stuff."

"I was much better too. Very flirty and funny."

We both laughed then returned to our dessert.

"I like that we're bad at dating," Carson said.

"Me too."

Chapter Thirty-Five

"You sound like crap."

"Thanks, Mal. Love you too."

"Seriously, Luz. You're sick."

I started to protest but a fit of coughing came and went, leaving me breathless and sweating. I'd been fighting it for days. I hated to agree with her, but I seemed to be losing the battle.

"I've told her to go home three times already."

"You're not the boss of me, Carson."

"Does she always revert to a child when she's sick?" he asked Mallie.

"Usually, yes." She grinned at him, then looked back to me. No smile for me though, only concern. I knew I must look as bad as I felt to get Mallie's concerned face.

"Fine, fine, fine. I'm going home and to bed. Y'all have to keep Ria for me. I don't want to give her my germs."

They both agreed and sent me on my way. I backtracked through the house, past the library, now organized. Past the dining room, the newly painted living room. I even peeked into Carson's apartment off the kitchen. He'd stripped the wallpaper here too. One of Mallie's guys was in there painting it today. I felt like a lazy slug abandoning ship and then another round of coughing doubled me over.

When I got to the cottage, I took cough medicine and crawled into bed. It knocked me right out, and I slept through lunch and into the afternoon. When I woke up, I felt human again. After a shower, I knew I couldn't go back to work even if I did feel better. I was dizzy and light-headed from the ten minutes under the hot water. So I went back to bed, this time with my laptop. I could at least get a few things off my to-do list while I rested the day away.

I pulled up my list, crossing off everything I could. I even added a few things, then crossed them off, too. I felt very accomplished by the time I got to the end. I started to close the file, then realized it had a second page. Scrolling down, I found a message I'd left for myself. *You need to reach out to Teo's family and try to make things right.*

I didn't remember adding it to my list but it was something I needed to do. On a whim, I pulled up the video messenger program on my computer and tapped on the only contact icon I had saved—Mateo's sister Tia. I'd added her as a contact when I got the computer, thankful she'd given me her username ages ago. I hadn't had the nerve to reach out to her since she'd told me what her parents thought. I was worried she thought the same. We'd never really been friends, but we'd at least been halfway friendly with each other. If she came over to her parents' way of thinking, I'd never gain any ground with them and, I worried, Ria would never know them as she grew up. So I waited, hoping the whole family was home on a Friday afternoon.

They were.

I panicked for a second as the program connected our computers. I hadn't talked to them since the day I had discovered they'd moved and then it was just Tia. It had been even longer since I'd talked to Mr. and Mrs. Baca—I'd never won them over to get to first name status and couldn't even think of them by any other names. I'd left them alone, letting them process everything in their own way.

"Hey, Luz. What's up?" It was Tia. Only Tia. She still sorta liked me so my panic faded.

"Hey, Tia. I just wanted to reach out and check on y'all. How's sunny Phoenix?"

She smiled and sat down in front of the computer. "We're all good. Are you in bed? Are you okay?"

"I'm okay. Caught myself a cold. I've been home resting. I woke up from a nap a bit ago and was feeling better so I thought I'd give you a call. How are your folks?"

162

"They're right here. Ask them yourself." She spoke to someone off screen, frowned at them and whispered angrily. I couldn't hear her, but it was clear she was bossing her parents into coming to talk to me. A chair was set down beside her then another one and finally, her parents came into frame, sitting on either side of her. They didn't look thrilled to see me. I paused, looking at them, wishing I could somehow fix what had gone wrong. Losing Teo shouldn't have driven them out of town and out of Ria's life. I didn't share my grief with them, didn't turn to them, and I should have. They shouldn't have laid any sort of blame on me though. We were all wrong. I couldn't fix it but I could at least be honest with them.

"Hey, y'all. You both look well." I paused and waited for them to say something but they didn't. "Anyway, I wanted to catch all of y'all up on some things."

"We already know how the trial went," Mrs. Baca said.

"Yes, I figured you did."

"Well, then," she said, starting to stand.

"Please—don't go. There's more." She sat reluctantly. I paused, then decided to go for it. Lay out everything. "I wanted y'all to know I'm not working at the RWB anymore. A friend and I have bought the old Tate House. We're turning it into a bed and breakfast. I'll text you our new address. Ria's doing really well. She's with Mallie right now, hopefully not getting my cold. Everyone around town misses all of you. When you come back for a visit, you'll be able to stay here, at the B and B. On me. Anytime you come to town."

"That's very nice of you, Luz," Mr. Baca said. Somehow, the way he said *nice* didn't sound very nice. It almost sounded like an insult.

"I know you aren't big fans of me right now. I know you think what happened is somehow my fault. Shoot, I know you think I got pregnant to trap Teo. I know you have high standards for your family that I will never reach. None of that matters though. We're family. We became family when Teo and I exchanged our vows and his death doesn't change that. We will always be connected. I hope you'll always remember. I care so much about each of you and Ria adores y'all. We miss you."

"Thank you, Luz," Mrs. Baca said, standing again. She still hadn't cracked. Neither had Mr. Baca. I was starting to think that even Jesus Himself couldn't make them soften their hard hearts.

"Please, I have one more thing to tell you. I don't think you'll be very happy to hear it but . . . shoot, you're not happy with me right now anyway. I wanted y'all to know I'm seeing someone. I didn't want it to get to y'all through gossip or rumors. I wanted you to hear it from me. He's a good man. He was widowed too, several years ago. He's helped me learn to—"

"That's enough. I'm done talking to her." Mrs. Baca stood a final time and stormed out of sight. Mr. Baca followed. Only Tia was left.

"I'm sorry, Luz. They're still so sad and so angry. I really thought they'd be better by now."

"It's not your fault, Tia. They have a right to grieve how they want."

"I'm glad you're seeing someone. My brother would want you to be happy. You are happy, aren't you?"

"I am, Tia. I really am."

Chapter Thirty-Six

I'd barely closed the laptop when Mallie came walking in.

"Where's my kid, Mal?"

"With your mom. I came to pack a bag for her. You've been ruled too germy to keep her tonight."

I laughed, then started coughing. Mallie watched me from the doorway. She was without her crutches today, her repaired knee still encased in a heavy brace. I'd kept an eye on her before my cold got the best of me. Even favoring her healing knee, she was ridiculously graceful. She'd been graceful on the crutches too. Mallie would never lose her dancer grace, I decided.

"Should you go to the doctor?"

"No. I feel better, I swear. I'll go take more medicine right now." I kicked myself free from the blankets on my bed and got up. "Here. Let me gather stuff up for Ria. Thanks for calling my mom."

"It was Carson's idea."

"Well, then tell him thanks for me."

"Thank him yourself. He needs to crash over here tonight. His place is full of fresh paint and tarps."

"I saw they were painting in his apartment. I didn't even think about where he'd sleep tonight. There are spare sheets there," I said, pointing to the built-in cabinets at the end of the hall. I didn't have to say anything else. Mallie and I always shared a brain. She got sheets, blankets, and a couple of pillows and made up the couch for Carson, finishing as I came into the room with an overnight bag for Ria.

Instead of taking it, Mallie sat down at my kitchen table. I sat across from her, waiting for her to tell me what she wanted to talk about.

"So."

"So what, Mal?"

"How's it feel to be dating again?"

I smiled. Always straight to the point, my best friend. One of the many things I loved about her. "I'm terrible at it but so is Carson."

"You're out of practice."

"Exactly what he said."

"So other than being terrible at it, how's it going?"

"Good. He's fun to hang out with. We could talk for hours."

"He's good looking too."

"You're married, Mal."

"I can still look," she said with a smile. "I'd have to be blind not to notice him."

"Yeah, he's not bad to look at. I'll admit it."

"He likes you. A lot."

"Maybe. I don't know."

"I know. The man has gone to the RWB to get you a burger and is stopping at the bakery to get you dessert. He likes you, Luz, and I can tell from how much you're blushing that you like him a lot, too."

"Maybe. I . . . is it too soon, Mallie?"

"Too soon for what? To fall for someone? Who knows? No one can answer that for you. Everyone lives life on a different timeline. Uncle Noah told me that. I figure as a preacher, a man with a direct line to God, he knows what he's talking about. You should talk to him."

"Yeah, maybe I should. I told Teo's family I was dating."

"Whoa. When?"

"Right before you got here. I called Tia on the video chat thing on the laptop."

"How'd they take the news?"

"Pretty much like you'd expect them to. They got mad. Madder, I guess. They were mad through the whole conversation. Tia's happy for me though. She said Mateo would want me to be happy."

166

"Well, she's right. He would. How the two of them came from those hotheads I'll never understand. Two of the most chill people in the world. Their parents could learn from them."

"You say that every time we talk about them. You're right though. I never understood it either. I never could make them like me either."

"Add me to the list. They never liked me. Or Tres."

"I'm not sure they like anyone really."

Mallie laughed and stood up. She grabbed the bag of Ria's stuff and headed to the door. "I'll hug you when you're well."

"Love you, Mallie Jo."

"Love you, too, Lucy Lou."

*****

"Dinner is served, milady," Carson said as he walked in not long after Mallie left. I was still in the dining room at the little table, with my laptop now, doing a little more work on my to-do list. Carson sat down the food and closed the laptop. "No more work. Dinner. Then some cold meds for you."

"You know, crashing here tonight puts you at risk for getting this cold too."

"I'll risk it."

"The mess in your apartment really that bad?"

"Not really. I'd rather hang out with you tonight."

I flushed and looked away, scooping up the laptop and carrying it back to my bedroom. I was glad Mallie had told me he was coming over with dinner. I'd had time to trade in my ratty pajamas for a clean sweatshirt and yoga pants. I still looked sick but at least I didn't look as rough as I had when Mallie had walked in.

Carson had burgers and fries set out when I came back. I spotted a bag from Abbott Bakery on the counter and resisted the urge to take a peek at dessert. It didn't matter what it was. It would be

167

good. Everything coming out of the bakery was amazing. Joy saw to it.

We ate in easy silence. It was nice to have food from the diner. It'd been weeks since I'd had one of my dad's burgers. Ria and I had been living off Thanksgiving leftovers and sandwiches. I knew she was getting sick of them and so was I. With all the pace of work on the house, though, I hadn't had time to do much grocery shopping or any cooking. I was touched Carson had called my mom, gotten Ria a germ-free place to sleep, and then brought me dinner. It had been a long time since someone had done that sort of stuff for me.

"Why are you taking care of me today?"

"Because you have a cold. Plus, you're pretty. I like doing nice things for pretty girls."

He kept talking but my brain checked out when he said I was pretty. I didn't feel pretty today. I felt sick and tired. I felt like a worn-out single mom who was a little too happy her kid was crashing at another house tonight.

"Luz . . . you okay?"

I shook my head, clearing the silly, happy haze the word *pretty* had conjured. "Sorry. What did you say?"

"Not important. Where'd you go?"

I hesitated and decided honesty was best. "My inner sixteen-year-old girl took over when you called me pretty. I couldn't hear anything over all of her squealing."

"Totally understand. My inner sixteen-year-old boy gets loud sometimes too."

"Oh yeah? What does he say?"

"The pretty girl thing a lot. Lately though he says I should kiss you."

I felt my face go hot but held his gaze. *His eyes are so green*, the silly sixteen-year-old whispered. "Wait until I'm not sick, okay?"

"I can do that," he said with a smile and a wink.

Chapter Thirty-Seven

I woke the next morning feeling much more human. Carson, sadly, had caught my cold. I made both of us breakfast, each with a side of cold meds. I made him promise to stay on the couch, gave him the TV remote, and headed across the backyard to get to work on the last of the wallpaper on the first floor—a study on the back of the house we were hoping to turn into a media room.

I didn't make it to the house though. Mom pulled up before I got there so I detoured to the driveway, reaching the little gate in the wrought-iron fence as she set Ria on the ground.

"Mama!" she screamed, running toward me. She stumbled, nearly fell, then barreled into me, almost knocking me down. She launched into a long story about everything she'd done last night. Her grandparents had spoiled her but I wasn't mad. They'd helped me out without a thought and I appreciated it. I told my mom exactly that when she walked up.

"It's no problem. Are you feeling better?" She put her hand on my forehead as she spoke. "You feel a little warm."

"I'm better. I took another dose of medicine maybe fifteen minutes ago. Carson's sick now. He's still sleeping on my couch so he can rest while everyone else works."

"He slept at your house?"

"He did, Mami. On the couch. They're working in his apartment."

She stared at me, pressing her lips into a thin line. Ria started to wiggle so I set her down and she went running across the big backyard. She had several toys scattered across the yellowed grass. She found a little ball and started kicking it around. It was her most recent obsession. Kicking things. Thankfully, a growing collection of Maria-sized soccer balls kept her focused on toys. Sadly, when she got worn out and cranky other things became a substitute. Things like furniture or me. I'd learned to keep balls around at all times.

"What's going on with you and this boy?" she finally asked.

"He's not a boy, Mom. He's a grown adult just like I am. We're business partners and friends."

"Your sister says you're dating him."

"Which sister?" I started planning to yell at someone immediately.

"Isabel."

"Isabel needs to not tell things that aren't hers to share." I regretted being snarky but Is should have kept her mouth shut. Mom should have heard this information from me first. "Isabel is right, though, Carson and I have been on two whole dates. Three if you count dinner at my kitchen table last night."

"I think it's too soon for you to be dating. What will Maria think? She barely remembers her father as it is."

"Mom, I'm not going to have this conversation with you. You can't tell me what to do with my love life or with Maria's life. You've got to let me make my own choices. I feel ready to date. Carson is a good man and he makes me happy. I haven't been happy in a long time. Let me be happy."

She looked at me again, still frowning but softer now.

"Okay. Come by the diner. Your father misses you." She hugged me quickly, then stepped away. "Don't work too hard today."

"I promise. Thank you. Love you."

"Love you, too," she said. She was gone in a second.

I turned my focus back on my wild child. She was kicking her ball through piles of leaves, stopping to throw the leaves up in the air. I glanced over at the house. None of Mallie's crew was here yet. I decided to set aside work for a bit longer and play with my kid.

*****

At lunch, I realized what else had been behind my mom's frown this morning. Ria's birthday was in four days. I'd been so busy, I'd forgotten my kid's birthday. I wasn't ready for Christmas either and it would be here in no time.

"Mallie, I'm taking the rest of the week off. I've got to deal with life stuff."

"What life stuff?" She didn't look up from her work. She was sprawled on the hallway floor, right leg straight out, caged in the brace. I watched as she carefully touched up the stain on the wainscoting in the hallway, dings and scuffs disappearing as she scooted herself along the floor.

"Your niece's birthday. Christmas. Grocery shopping."

"Okay. Go."

"I don't have all the wallpaper stripped on the first floor and Carson's sick."

"We finished up a job the other day. I've got a few guys wanting some more work before we shut down for the holiday. I'll get them on it."

"You sure?"

She finally looked up at me. "This is what you hired me to do, silly. You don't have to be killing yourself over here every day. It saves you money, but you still need to handle all the other stuff in your life. Go. Plan Ria's birthday party. Buy me something fancy for Christmas. I've got this."

"You're the best. I'm out of here. I'm buying you a fancy pair of high heels for Christmas."

"Don't you dare. My doctor has forbidden those."

"Got it. A new tool belt then. Something in pink with sparkles."

"You think I wouldn't use it, but I would rock a pink tool belt."

I laughed at her as I left. I never thought I'd be buying Mallie Jo, the ballet dancer, a tool belt for Christmas. Never thought I'd be rehabbing an old house turned bed and breakfast either. Never thought I'd be happy a man was spending life in prison. Never thought I'd be

172

dating again. This year had been full of things I never thought would happen to me. Some good. Some bad. I was glad the year was ending but was actually excited to see what the new one would bring.

Chapter Thirty-Eight

"Dr. Bell. Do you have a bit of time?" I waited in the doorway of his office for an answer, halfway in the deserted hallway, halfway in the office. The church was empty like I'd expected it to be. Thursday afternoons weren't really big days in the world of the Rio Verde Baptist Church.

"Luz," Dr. Bell said. He stood and came around his desk, giving me a hug. "I've always got time for you. Come on in. Sit."

I took one of the chairs in front of his desk, remembering sitting here as a teen, Mallie beside me. We'd gotten in trouble for interrupting choir practice. The choir director had wanted us banished from the church. Dr. Bell had spent more time calming him down than he spent scolding us.

"What did you want to talk about, Luz?"

"Well, sir," I stopped. I still wasn't sure I wanted to talk to him about this, but Mallie had made it sound like a good idea. "When do you think it's appropriate to start dating after the death of a spouse?"

"That's a loaded question. The short answer is, I don't think there is an 'appropriate' time. There isn't a timeline for grief, Luz. Your heart doesn't heal on a set schedule. For some people, there is no right time. Some hearts never heal from such a loss. Others are open to love again much sooner." He smiled at me across the desk, knitting his hands together. I always saw Will in him when he smiled. The same coffee skin, same brown eyes filled with kindness and caring each time he smiled an understanding smile. Dr. Bell always made me feel better and understood, even if we only spoke for a moment.

"That's what I thought you'd say."

"You still seem uneasy. Why?"

"I'm worried about what people will say."

"Why?"

"Because everyone loved Mateo so much. Everyone respected him. I don't want to color his memory by . . . when I . . . if I . . ."

"Have you started seeing someone, Luz?"

"Yes, sir."

"Do you enjoy spending time with this man? Does he make you happy?"

"Yes, sir."

"Then it doesn't matter what people say."

"I feel guilty. I feel like I should still be sad."

Dr. Bell sighed and leaned back in his chair. He thought for a moment, eyes lifted up toward Heaven. "Luz, people never anticipate the bad parts of life. We don't plan for them. Sometimes, though, after a terrible and sudden loss, perspective changes and a person can start to only anticipate badness. It can be nearly impossible to see the good parts of life. I think your loss did that to you. I also think you're starting to find your way back to your old mindset. You wouldn't be here talking to me about this if you weren't. The old Luz, the Luz I've known for years, wouldn't care what people said so long as she was happy."

"Good point."

"Go be happy, Luz. Don't worry about anything else."

I stood and thanked him, earning myself another hug. As I left the church, I felt better than I had in months and months. Everything Dr. Bell had said, every single word, had lifted my worries. He was right. I was finding my way back to myself and it felt so good.

*****

A week later and I'd gotten a lot better at balancing work on the house and life stuff. Since my talk with Dr. Bell, I'd gotten all my Christmas shopping done and put on Ria's birthday party. Of course, I'd had help. As it turned out, my parents weren't sitting back watching me. They were waiting for me to ask for help. Mom helped me pull together Ria's party, hosting it at their house since my construction zone wasn't exactly kid-safe. She'd even reached out to Mateo's parents. She had, as Mallie would have said, a come-to-Jesus talk with them. I couldn't get her to tell me what she'd said, but they'd video chatted with Maria on her birthday and sent her a thoughtful present. I knew I still had a long road to go with them, but Mom had at least gotten them to bend a little.

While I'd been busy getting back on top of my life, Carson had been exploring the attics of both houses. He'd found a wealth of Christmas decorations. He'd decorated the outside of the houses and put up a Christmas tree in the cottage. I'd had to talk him out of decorating the big house. Mallie's crew had been thankful. They'd stared in terror when he'd tried to decorate the first floor. Every room aside from the kitchen was in the process of getting the floor refinished. I'd seen the relief in their faces when I'd shut down his plan. Outside decorations would have to do this year.

"What is with you and Christmas?" I asked him as I helped him carry boxes of garland and ornaments back to the attic.

"I grew up in the French Quarter. Everything, and I mean *everything*, was decorated. Lamp posts. Streetcars. Every shop front, garden gate, and balcony railing had garland or wreaths or lights on it. It was my favorite time of year. Everything was transformed. I loved it."

"Aww, you're like a little kid. It's adorable."

"I'm not adorable. I'm very manly and handsome."

"You're the biggest fan of Christmas I've ever met." I teased him more as we put away the decorations he hadn't used. Eventually, we started talking about all holidays. He asked what my favorite was, and he wasn't surprised when I said it was Thanksgiving.

By the time we'd gotten everything put away, Mallie's crew had knocked off for the day, leaving us with an empty house. We split up, each going home. Tonight was date night. Ria was already with Joy and Will for the night, giving them a good taste of parenthood, I was sure. Probably a good bit of screaming was going on, plus lots of throwing things unless Joy somehow managed to work her magic a second time and convinced her to stop screaming. She'd been in a mood all day. I felt sort of bad but only a little. I was excited to go out to dinner tonight. After talking with Dr. Bell, I wanted to go out for dessert after dinner. Dessert at the most popular ice cream shop in town, right on the square. I didn't want to go to out of the way spots anymore. I didn't want to hide. I was happy. I was moving forward. I knew the old church ladies—Mallie's dad called them the blue hairs—I knew they'd talk. Plenty of people my own age would talk. Dr. Bell had made me realize it didn't matter what they thought. It didn't matter one bit.

Chapter Thirty-Nine

"Ice cream?"

Carson stopped in the dark parking lot and gave me a look. I was learning his looks. This one was asking if I was serious. I got it a lot. He questioned me on stuff all day, mostly just to get a rise out of me.

"Yes, I'm serious."

"You do realize," he started, pausing to open my door. He hurried around the front of my car, getting in and starting the engine. I waited while he turned the radio down and the heater up. "You do realize it's supposed to start snowing in a couple of hours."

On the two-lane highway running beside the restaurant, a TXDOT truck went by, salting the road in anticipation of the forecasted snow. He grinned and pointed to the truck so I pulled up the weather app on my phone.

"See. It's only thirty-six. Not too cold. Plus, you've lived in Alaska. You should be more cold-tolerant than this." He looked at me and pretended to shiver. I rolled my eyes at him. "Ice cream and hot chocolate maybe?"

"Deal. Where to?"

"The square. To Baylor's Ice Cream Shop."

"The place diagonal from Joy's?"

"Uh huh."

"Pretty popular place."

"It's very good."

"You ready for people to know?"

We'd talked about it on our second date. Rio Verde was a small town. People knew each other's business. Everyone's lives were connected and intertwined. We'd purposely been going to places in other nearby towns for our date nights. It was awfully early to invite the whole town into the new world we were building. I didn't answer him, not right away. I watched the countryside fly past as we drove back to town. It was dark but not. The sky had a lightness to it. There was snow in the clouds. It was exciting. The first snow of the winter always was.

I finally looked away from the clouds when we turned onto the square. It was busy. The RWB had a good crowd. So did the Italian place at the opposite end of the street. Several other businesses had lights on, customers visible through the front windows. There were Christmas lights in all the trees and in the gazebo in the square. We circled it once, then parked in front of the bakery. The store was dark but the lights on the second floor were on. Joy and Will were probably eagerly waiting for us to come get Ria.

"Luz, you sure you're ready to go public?"

"I am." He turned off the car and I caught his hand. "Carson, I want you to know I'm all in on this. Our relationship. Our business. Everything."

Carson smiled and cupped my face with his hand.

"That is very good to know because I am too. I wasn't looking for any of this but I sure am happy I found it."

"Me too."

He leaned over and touched my lips with his once, then smiled at me before giving me a second kiss. I was game for a third but a chorus of sudden giggles reminded us we were on a public street. We quickly climbed out of the car and headed toward the ice cream shop, ignoring the continued giggles from the teen girls trailing behind us. When Carson offered me his hand, I took it without a second thought. I wasn't letting go. Not ever.

*****

"You're staring."

I looked at the wall I was supposed to be painting, then looked at Mallie. She was watching me, a you-like-a-boy smile on her face.

"I don't know what you're talking about."

"Liar. You totally know what I'm talking about. You know who I'm talking about, too."

I focused on my work, transforming the bare plaster wall with each stroke of my brush. The soft blue was my favorite wall color so far. It would make the tower sitting room on the second floor feel like a tree house. I tried to ignore Mallie and stay focused, but Carson walked by the doorway again, humming a Christmas song. My eyes followed him and I smiled. I couldn't stop myself.

"You're doing it again."

"Oh my gosh, fine. Yes. I'm staring. I can't help it." I put down my pain brush and faced her. "I just kind of want to kiss him all the time now."

She glanced over, raised one eyebrow, and smirked. "So you're kissing him now?" Laughter danced on the edges of her words. She'd get me laughing before long, I knew it. Her humor was infectious.

"He started it."

Mallie tried to stay focused, staring at the wall like I had done. She shook with suppressed laughter though, finally giving in, her laughs filling the room. We were both doubled over, nearly out of breath, when Carson appeared in the doorway again.

"Are y'all okay?"

"It's all Mallie's fault. She's so unprofessional."

Mallie shoved me, then smiled at Carson. He shook his head and returned to his own project.

"What is he doing out there?" Mallie asked.

"I have no idea. The wallpaper in one of the bedrooms maybe?"

We returned to our painting, working in silence. I worked on the edges, carefully cutting in around all the wood trim. Mallie worked behind me with the roller. In the quiet, I could hear work sounds echoing up the stairs from the first floor. A sander running, another

180

room getting the floor refinished. Sudden bursts of laughter. Occasional snippets of music from a distant radio. Christmas music.

"So you really like him, then?"

"I do, Mal. I wasn't looking for any of this. This house. This business. Carson. God brought it to me anyway. Or brought me to it. The past few months have reset me. He's a big part of it."

"Why?"

"He's walked ahead of me. Through this kind of loss. He makes me hopeful. He makes me happy."

"Good. I want you happy."

"I am."

Epilogue

Five years later

To borrow a line from my favorite book, *Jane Eyre*, "Reader, I married him."

"Mom! Lucas took my sandwich!"

I didn't move, the sunshine felt too good. A shadow suddenly fell across my face and I opened my eyes, my daydream about *Jane Eyre* gone. The reality of life with Carson was better than the fictional Mr. Rochester anyway.

"What, Maria?"

Maria glared down at me. Eight years old and I could still see her at three. She'd move a certain way or make a certain face and I'd see her as she'd been when Carson joined our family.

"Lucas took my sandwich."

"Lucas isn't my responsibility. Go tell your aunt Joy. He's her kid."

She huffed and stomped off. She ruined my rest so I pushed myself up. Not an easy task at seven months pregnant. I looked around me, the wide meadow scattered with people, with my family. Joy sat nearby, in a similar condition at six months pregnant. Her little boy, Lucas, raced between us, chased by Ria. He held a plastic bag with a sandwich in it, laughing as he ran from her. There were plenty of sandwiches to go around but there was no point explaining it to them.

"Your kid," I said to her.

"I know. God's paying me back for my childhood." She laughed, pushing herself up. She looked like she was smuggling a basketball under her shirt. I'd blown past that look at five months. I rubbed my belly, the baby kicking. This kid was going to be big. The doctor had already confirmed it. I wouldn't be getting up without help.

I looked around more, found Tres and Mallie and Will. Tres and Will were tossing a Frisbee back and forth, stopping to let the little boy Mallie held toss the plastic disc. Matthew—Matty—their adopted little boy. Matty had joined the family just over a year ago. They'd gotten to foster him when he was just a week old, but they'd had to wait for his troubled mother to sign away her rights before they could adopt him. Poor kid had started out life rough, born addicted to cocaine. You couldn't tell now though. He was a thriving two-year-old.

Speaking of two-year-olds . . . I scanned the field again, finding Carson. He was near the edge of the meadow, looking out over the Alaska forest with our daughter in his arms. Lily, nearly the exact same age as Matty, was a doll. I was biased, but she had gone on this hike in a princess dress so I stood by calling her a doll. Ria was quickly growing into a real tomboy. Lily was going to be our princess. Mallie had already suggested ballet classes for her. I had a feeling someone was going to follow in her auntie's pointe shoes.

Now that I had done a head count, I laid back down. I wasn't going to waste a minute of resting time. I never got to just lay in the sunshine these days. I thought about the bed and breakfast back home. The Tate House, now The Green River Inn, was in good hands. Carson's sister had come up from New Orleans with her new husband to watch over the place for us. She'd insisted, saying it was her present to us for our anniversary.

The big family trip had been Carson's idea. We'd come to Alaska on our honeymoon. He wanted to come back for this anniversary and bring our family. With all of us running our own businesses, big vacations weren't something we did. He reasoned it would be easier to go together than for each of us to take individual trips. I hadn't really gotten on board with his logic, but I loved the idea of a big trip with everyone so I'd agreed.

Mallie had left Kevin and her dad taking care of the restoration business. They were crazy busy, working on three restoration projects, but Tio Jonah had made her leave anyway. Mallie had done well too, only calling him a dozen times in the three days we'd been gone. Tres was the least worried of all of us. He'd left the farm in the hands of a neighbor. It wasn't time to cut hay yet, so all he really had to do was check the irrigation and feed the dogs.

Joy had left the bakery with her mom and Lane and the rest of the bakery staff. There was a wedding while we were gone, but pregnancy had chilled Joy out and she wasn't worried at all. It was a strange side of Joy we were all still getting used to. She'd taken my idea though and bought the hardware store next door, expanding the bakery. They now had a coffee shop and served breakfast five days a week. She and Will also expanded their apartment too; gaining some much-needed living space for their rapidly growing family.

The B and B was doing well too. We were booked consistently with both regular guests and events. We'd become one of the hot spots for weddings and other fancy parties. Like Will and Joy, Carson and I had done some renovations. We'd given up the single car garage on the guesthouse, turning it into a master bedroom with a much-needed second bathroom. While we were up here, Jonah was exploring our attic, looking at adding a bedroom and bathroom up there, too. We were hoping to move Ria up there and use her room for the new baby. We were also talking about turning part of the attic on the Inn into a big suite—possibly a honeymoon suite with a bedroom, sitting room, and a big bathroom. That would have to wait until our house was finished. Finding places for the kids took precedence.

So many changes in five years. It was hard to grasp it all. Looking back over it all made it seem so huge.

"Need a hand?" I opened my eyes again, this time to both Joy and Mallie. Mallie held out a hand to me and I took it, letting her tug me to my feet.

"Thanks, Mal. I thought I was going to have to stay there all day."

"That was a long hike," Joy said. "I was enjoying napping in the grass."

"Me too."

Mallie rolled her eyes at us. "Lazy, pregnant women."

Joy shoved her and I stuck my tongue out at her.

"Y'all ready to head back?" Carson. He yelled out to all of us, backpack already on his shoulders, Lily in her carrier on his chest. I had to admit, seeing him carrying her was kind of hot.

"Stop it," Mallie said, giving me a gentle shove. "Looking at him like that is how you got in this shape."

I burst out laughing, Joy laughing too. She had a point though.

Mallie gathered the blankets Joy and I had been napping on and shoved them in another backpack that she put over her own shoulders. Carson practically bounded out of the clearing, leading us back down the trail.

"Ugh. Who brought him along?" I said.

"You did when you married him," Joy said. We fell in line, following Carson and Will as they led the way, Lucas and Ria on their heels. Mallie and Tres brought up the rear with Matty.

"He's your best friend. This is all your fault," I told her, pressing my hand to the small of my back. Hiking probably hadn't been the best idea. I saw Joy do the same thing. We would probably have to skip any other hikes Carson had planned.

She laughed at me and pointed out I'd said the same thing when I was in mid-labor with Lily. I hadn't stayed mad once I'd held her.

"You okay, babe?" Carson asked, pausing and looking back at us.

"Yeah, I'm good. Just take it slow." He smiled, waiting for me to catch up to him.

"Maybe no more hiking," he said, giving me a hug and a kiss.

"Maybe no more hiking. He's heavy," I said cradling my bump. We didn't know if it was a boy. He was hoping for another girl. He was having a blast being a dad to two little girls. I had a feeling

185

though this one was a boy. I'd already decided he was our last, too. We couldn't add on to our house anymore. We didn't have any more room.

Carson couldn't handle walking as slow as me for long, quickly returning to the lead with Will. The trail was just as beautiful on the way down as it had been coming up. It took us through a thick forest, trees hemming in the trail, small meadows appearing suddenly, giving us a peek of sky and usually a display of wildflowers. The kids were racing up and down the trail, running past everyone only to get distracted by something and fall behind. The guys kept an eye on them, trusting Carson's wilderness experience to keep us all safe. He was doing great too. On our first day, he'd taken Tres and Will fishing far outside of the city on the Tanana River. A pair of bears had appeared and made Tres and Will want to sprint back the car. Carson had taken charge and guided them up a trail away from the bears, circling around them to safety. Now Carson could do no wrong as far as those two were concerned.

Today we'd traded in our pair of rental cars for a big van and started the drive through the wilderness to Seward. Even though we could make it in a day, Carson had it planned for three days so we could make a lot of stops. He assured us we'd want to. He'd been right, too. We'd made it to Denali National Park and no further. Alaska was about as different from the Texas high plans as a place could be. Looking around, seeing all the beauty, was a feast for my eyes and mind. There were more trees and green in a square mile than in all of Rio Verde combined.

I stopped at one of the little meadows and sat on a bolder by the trail, looking up toward Heaven, closing my eyes as the sun warmed my face. I felt him watching, felt Mateo keeping an eye on his girls. I felt them all. Lena. Mallie's mom. Even Joy's grandparents. All the family we had lost was up there, watching over us.

I opened my eyes when Mallie called my name. She and Tres had passed me. They stood in the trail, waiting for me to come along. As I pushed myself off the stone and hurried to join my family, I sent a quick prayer toward Heaven, thanking the Lord for the guiding hand that had brought us all together.

God things. Every little piece of the puzzle that had put our family together. God things, every one.

They were all around us, adding to the life He'd planned for us, building something more beautiful than I could ever have imagined.

Wonderful, surprising God things.

About the Author

A few years ago, a chance visit to a new church changed the path of Elise Phillips' life. After many years away from the church, Elise found her way back to the Lord. With the support of her friends, family, and church, finally she chased her writing dream. First, by getting a master's degree in Creative Writing from Southern New Hampshire University. Second, by turning her thesis project into a novel. Elise firmly believes that your talent is your gift from God and what you do with it is your gift to Him. Though currently working as a graphic designer, Elise hopes to one day be able to fully dedicate her life to writing stories filled with faith and God's love. In her spare time, Elise tries to find time to pursue her many hobbies, including photography, knitting, and above all else, reading.

A fifth generation Texan, Elise calls the top of Texas home, residing in Amarillo with her fur kids, Ice and CC. Elise is excited for the new adventures that writing is bringing into her life and can't wait to see what will come next.

www.ingramcontent.com/pod-product-compliance
Lightning Source LLC
Chambersburg PA
CBHW020908180626
46816CB00007BA/2297